GIRL LEFT BEHIND

C.J. CROSS

LIQUID MIND PUBLISHING

ALSO BY C.J. CROSS

Dana Gray Mysteries

Girl Left Behind

Girl on the Hill

Girl in the Grave

Stay up to date with C.J. Cross's new releases and download her **free** Dana Gray Prequel, *Girl Awakened* by heading to the link:

PROLOGUE

H<small>E TOOK A FINAL DRAG FROM HIS CIGARETTE AS HIS PREY APPROACHED.</small> Holding the smoke in his lungs, he savored the tranquil feeling that washed over him. This was it—the calm before the storm. His first kill. It had to be perfect.

Letting the sound of their unsuspecting voices center him, he exhaled, stubbing out the cigarette butt as he listened in on what would be the last pleasant conversation the couple would ever have.

"I don't know, James . . . I see potential here, but it would mean uprooting our daughter. Do you really think it's worth altering her life like this?"

"Renee, you know as well as I do our girl is exceptional. I have every faith that Dana will adjust. Besides, doesn't everything feel life altering at thirteen?"

"I suppose you're right."

"You know I am. And don't forget Dana is half the reason we're doing this."

Curiosity ate at him as the silence following the exchange between the couple dragged on. It had him moving to the peephole in the flimsy motel door. He knew he shouldn't risk it, but he couldn't help himself.

This kill was special and so were the victims. They hadn't been chosen at random. No, each life collected held special meaning. These two even more because they would be his first.

Holding his breath, he gazed through the peephole, getting a glimpse at the stars of his show. They didn't know it yet, but they were about to earn a special place in history.

The couple embraced each other just outside the door, staring lovingly into each other's eyes after sharing a tender kiss. It was their love and devotion that had won them this coveted spot over so many other contenders.

The woman wore an emerald silk blouse that emphasized the green in her hazel eyes. The man wore a brown tweed blazer almost the exact shade of his hair. They would look gorgeous laid out on the stage he'd set for them. For a moment he wondered about the daughter they spoke of. What did she look like? Did she take after her mother or her father, or was she an equal blend of the two? Maybe one day he would have a chance to find out.

Visions flashed through his mind of finding the girl and bringing her into the fold. With enough time he could make her see why her parents had been chosen, why it was such an honor, one maybe they could share together in the future. Clamping the lid on his excitement, he pushed the thoughts to a dark corner of his mind to revisit later. He had more pressing matters to focus on now.

The work had been done. Now all that was left to do was to wait for the show to begin. Stepping back from the door, he glanced one last time at the hotel room. The last one the couple would ever see. Excitement bubbled up as he stared at the pristine red and gold carpet. The pattern of starbursts called to him, the fibers aching to absorb the blood of his sacrifice.

Whispers too low for him to interpret were exchanged outside the door before he heard the key slip into the lock. His heart raced as the doorknob twisted, sealing the couple's fate. There was no going back now.

He gripped the camera in his trembling hands, willing himself to hold steady. He didn't want to miss this—the priceless expressions on his victims' faces as they realized their destiny and the fact that there was no escaping it.

1

"SHEP, OVER HERE!"

Jake Shepard nodded to his steely-haired superior before donning latex gloves and blue crime scene booties. SSA Tom Cramer had been the one to call Jake to the scene. It might not be textbook procedure by Bureau standards, but such behavior wasn't unusual between the two men. Jake and the savvy special agent had always shared a unique working relationship thanks to the unbreakable bond of brotherhood the Army afforded.

Even though Jake's days in uniform were behind him, he appreciated the camaraderie, nonetheless. Having Cramer take him under his wing had made the transition to civilian life a bit easier, especially since joining the FBI hadn't been the means to an end that Jake had hoped for.

Thanks to the nature of the covert special forces missions he'd served on in the military, he still had much to atone for. And from the looks of the crime scene he was standing in, he'd get to do a bit more of that today.

"Third one," Cramer said, shaking his head at the gruesome scene as Jake approached.

Sadly, Jake wasn't as shocked as he should have been by the lifeless bodies. It was the pentagram and antique glass vials that piqued his interest.

"Same MO?" he asked as he made his way toward the large pentagram sketched between the twin hotel beds.

"Seems that way," Cramer replied.

Jake's eyes scanned the occult symbol on the floor. It stood out boldly against the pale blues and yellows of the carpet pattern. Though it had been some time since it'd dried, there was no doubt in Jake's mind that the pentagram had been drawn in blood. Just like the other two.

He crouched lower, examining the way the blood had seeped into the carpet fibers. His mind flashed back to the two previous crime scenes he'd visited in the past few weeks, then to the present bodies laid out on the twin beds. They lay motionless, their hands folded over their chests, eyes closed, hair and clothing neatly arranged. If it weren't for the strange glass vials in their hands, he would've thought they were sleeping.

Apparently, that was the mistake a member of hotel housekeeping made at the first crime scene. But this was number three. Word was spreading.

DC might be a big city, but gossip was an artform here. Jake heard his uncle's voice in his head. *Lies spread faster than the devil's radio.*

Growing up in rural Nevada had left Jake with a plethora of unique euphemisms; ones he kept to himself thanks to his hard-learned lessons in the military. The Army taught him to conform or be cast out. And Jake had been cast out enough for one lifetime.

"He gets an A plus for consistency," Jake said, noting the killer's signature—the pentagram and glass vial in each victim's hands. "Any word from toxicology?"

Cramer shook his head. "Preliminary findings are the same as the other two. Vials are empty of trace, but we're still waiting for a full work up."

Jake sighed. "This makes three. It's officially a serial. Guess that means we're passing this off to BAU?"

"Not just yet," Cramer murmured.

A crime scene tech piped up. "But that's protocol. The Behavioral Analysis Unit is specially equipped to handle a scene like this. Unless you think this is a copycat situation?"

Cramer's nostrils flared as he stalked toward the green tech. Stopping short, he towered over the young man, who at least had the sense to cower under Cramer's stony glare.

"What I *think* is that you should do your job and get Agent Shepard up to speed on the scene," Cramer snapped, before storming toward the hotel room door.

Jake heard his boss mutter a few choice words under his breath as he ducked under the police tape and disappeared down the hall. He was clearly frustrated, and Jake didn't blame him. They now had six dead bodies and zero leads.

"What'd I say?" the tech asked, his face noticeably paler after an up-close and personal encounter with the gruff older agent.

"Nothing," Jake assured him. "It was a fair question. But when you've been doing this job as long as Cramer has, it's not a necessary one. At least not if you want to stay on his good side," he added with a wink.

The tech nodded.

"So, what've you got for me?" Jake asked, pulling out his notebook to take notes.

The tech began rattling off the details pertinent to the case.

"Two victims, DOA. Cassie Owens, twenty-eight, Tyson Kline, thirty-two. Cause of death currently unknown. Awaiting toxicology report."

Jake had already assessed most of this himself, but he let the eager tech continue, estimating time of death and other clinical information. This was a good teaching moment and there was no better place to learn than on the job. It wasn't until the tech got to the absurd title assigned to the killer that Jake stopped him.

"The Romeo and Juliet Killer?" Jake's dark eyebrows furrowed with disapproval. "That's what we're going with?"

The tech shrugged. "I didn't come up with it."

Grunting, Jake flipped his notebook closed, beginning to see why

Cramer needed a moment. This was the part Jake hated most. The fame and notoriety that would come along with deeming these murders serial ... it would be a media circus. Most of the time, that was exactly what these sick, murderous sociopaths expected. And one thing Jake hated was doing what was expected.

Thinking outside the box had saved his life a time or two. Why stop now?

"Thanks," Jake said, excusing himself. "Come find me if you have anything new."

Outside, Jake found Cramer hunched over the hood of his black SUV, studying something on his cell phone, a lit cigarette dangling from his lips.

"I thought you quit," Jake called as he walked over.

Cramer straightened. "So did I. Take a look at this."

Jake examined the phone Cramer handed over, frowning as he read the email. He read the same line twice to make sure he wasn't seeing things. *Dr. Gray. Smithsonian Occult History and Artifacts department.*

"What the hell is this?" Jake demanded.

"It's a directive from the powers that be."

"What does that mean?"

"It means from now on, you'll be working this case with a partner."

Jake worked his jaw, clenching down hard against the painful memories that began flooding back to him. "I don't do partners, Cramer. You know that."

"I know you prefer to work alone, but we've got nothing and let's face it, this isn't our typical case."

"You're right, it isn't. And adding some librarian I need to babysit isn't going to make it any easier."

"Listen, Shep, my hands are tied. The Bureau wants a consult on this one. Apparently, this witch doctor has helped us out before. Just set up a meeting and get me a lead before the media turns this into a three-ring circus."

Jake leaned back against the SUV with a sudden urge to take up smoking. It was either that or hit something, because Cramer was right. They were out of their depth here. Gang bangers, drug trafficking, terrorist cells, missing persons; that he was prepared for. But some satanic, pentagram-painting psycho? It wasn't a mind he was eager to explore.

That was the trouble, though. They had nothing. No leads. No way to track down this killer. No way to stop more innocent lives from being snuffed out. Sighing, Jake rubbed his temples, knowing once again, his sense of duty would make it impossible to ignore the Bureau's order to chase down every lead—even ones as crazy as talking to some "witch doctor" who probably never left the Smithsonian's rare books department.

"Fine," he muttered. "But I highly doubt some librarian is going to crack this case wide open."

"So do I, but we're not here to make assumptions. The job is to investigate every possible option until we uncover the truth."

"I know the drill," Jake muttered. He was expected to follow orders like a good soldier. It seemed there was no escaping the Army. On days like this, he felt like he'd merely traded one uniform for another. Sure, his Brooks Brothers suits fit a hell of a lot better than his multicam combat fatigues, but the jobs weren't much different—do what you're told, don't ask questions.

A need for justice had always driven Jake. It was one of the reasons he'd enlisted in the Army. But now, at the FBI, his desire ran deeper. He needed to do more than fulfill his patriotic duty and protect civil liberties. He owed a life debt and the best way to repay it seemed to be saving as many lives as he could. Otherwise, the guilt of being spared when others had not was too much to bear.

Shaking off his dark thoughts, Jake handed the phone back to his boss. "I guess I've got an appointment with the witch doctor."

2

"DR. GRAY?"

Dana Gray's head lifted as she reluctantly pulled herself from her work. Looking up from the ancient tome she'd been deciphering, she blew at the chocolate brown bangs hanging in her eyes. Annoyed, she smoothed back the stubborn strands that had escaped her haphazard bun and added another pen into the fray to hold them in place.

Pushing her magnified readers into her hair, Dana replaced them with her regular prescription lenses as she waited for the world around her to come back into focus. The dark head of Dana's intern timidly poked into her office.

"Oh, here you are." Claire awkwardly halted at the door, wringing her hands. "I'm sorry to interrupt, Dr. Gray, but you have a visitor."

"A visitor?" Dana forgot to hide the shock in her voice. She couldn't help it. In her line of work, visitors were rare. But that was the nature of the game when studying ancient history. All her subjects existed in the past tense. Some not at all. At least that's what mainstream society wanted to believe. But Dana believed there was more to the world than what most minds were comfortable accepting. That was why she'd dedicated her life to studying the occult. *Well, one of the reasons.*

Dana readjusted her glasses, which were already sliding down her nose. "Why didn't you page me?"

"I did," Claire rebuked, her clear blue eyes blinking behind her black cat-eye frames.

Dana's eyes flitted to the clear green pager on her antique desk. The outdated gadget looked other-worldly against the ornate carvings and artifacts on the polished fifteenth century desk. She knew it was impractical, but it had been the last gift her father gave her, and she couldn't part with it.

The display flashed, showing two missed pages. "Oh. So you did." Dana pushed her glasses up into her hair, tangling them with her readers as she rubbed her eyes. "Sorry. I was making some headway with these Nordic Grimoires. I must've been so engrossed I didn't hear your page."

"That's why most of modern society prefers cellphones," Claire replied, her tone factual.

Dana felt the corners of her lips lift. In the two years they'd been working together, she'd come to enjoy the girl's quirky personality. If it was possible, Claire was even more socially awkward than Dana. Although Dana preferred to think of herself as effectively concise, rather than socially inept. It wasn't her fault if most people she encountered didn't appreciate her honesty. It said more about their own insecurities than hers.

Dana clipped her pager to her belt and looked pointedly at Claire. "I own a cellphone. I just prefer not to bring it down to the stacks." She found it a distraction that took her out of the world she immersed herself in when she was among her books. Besides, the cell service this deep in the library was atrocious. But she was getting off subject. "Who's here to see me?"

Claire looked uncomfortable again. "An FBI agent."

"Really?" Dana felt her eyebrows rise. "Did he say why?"

"Nope. Only that he was here to speak to the 'witch doctor'," Claire muttered, her painted black fingernails emphasizing her air quotes.

Dana's cheeks burned. She was well aware of her horrible nickname, but most people had the decency to use it behind her back.

"Maybe you should tell this FBI agent that I'm not available," she said haughtily.

"I don't think that's gonna work."

"Why not?"

Claire shrugged. "He just looks like the type who doesn't take no for an answer, if you know what I mean."

She did. One didn't get to be head curator at the Smithsonian without knowing how to play the game, but Dana preferred working with the dead. They were more predictable. Having dedicated much of her life to studying rituals of death, Dana often found she didn't have patience for the living. But she was trying to make an effort these days. Mostly, for Claire's sake. She loved that she'd found such a dedicated intern, but Dana didn't want the girl to turn out like she had. Claire deserved a chance at a normal life.

Deciding it was best to gain as much information as possible about her visitor, Dana quizzed her intern further so she could be prepared for her apparently inevitable meeting. "What else did you notice?"

"About Secret Agent Man?" Claire's painted lips twitched into a momentary smirk, the deep cherry hue of her lipstick reminding Dana of a splash of blood in the snow. "He's hot. Like hot enough to melt a popsicle in a freezer, hot."

Dana laughed, caught off guard by her normally reserved intern's enthusiasm. "Wow. That's some description."

"Best one I've had all day," a gruff voice retorted.

Dana's attention was drawn to the man in an expensive-looking suit who unexpectedly darkened her doorway. Clearing his throat, he grinned at Claire, making the young girl blush. "Thanks for that, by the way. And you were right about me not taking no for an answer."

"Excuse me," Dana interrupted. "You need permission to be on this level of the library."

"I swear I told him to wait upstairs," Claire squeaked.

The man pulled out a badge and strode forward. "I have permission. Special Agent Jake Shepard. FBI."

3

Jake extended his hand, firmly gripping the woman's cool palm as his preconceived notions of the "witch doctor" vanished. He still hated the idea of having a partner. He didn't make a habit of relying on others for help, but he certainly didn't mind the company of a beautiful woman from time to time. And this woman, with her soft, supple frame, dark hair and even darker eyes was the epitome of beauty.

She was not at all who he'd been expecting, but Jake was pleasantly surprised the witch doctor looked nothing like the decrepit windbag he'd imagined being saddled with.

"Doctor Dana Gray," she said, returning his firm grip.

"So you're the witch doctor, huh?"

"It's not a nickname I appreciate," she replied, standing taller.

"Fair enough." Jake had earned his share of unflattering call signs in the Army as a private. More than a few he hadn't been fond of stuck around long enough to rub him the wrong way. He made a mental note to do his best to leave "witch" off the good doctor's name. It shouldn't be too hard considering she looked like all of his adolescent librarian fantasies come true with those glasses pushed up into her messy brown hair.

Refocusing, he gestured for Dr. Gray to take a seat. She remained standing. Another point for the good doctor. Jake contained his smirk. He loved a challenge. "I was told you'd be able to assist with an ongoing investigation."

She blinked those big brown eyes at him. "Assist the FBI?"

"That's right."

"I'm sorry but this is the first I'm hearing of it."

Jake swore under his breath, not at all surprised the Bureau had sent him in blind. This wouldn't be the first time, nor the last. The case-loads were many and the manpower never enough. "I apologize for the unannounced visit. You should've been sent a briefing."

Pulling up a chair, he took a seat at the giant old desk piled high with dusty leather-bound books. He was puzzled by the absence of electronics in the room. And was she wearing a pager?

Maybe the Bureau *had* emailed Dr. Gray a memo. Little good it would do if she was stuck in the Stone Age. Dr. Gray's office reminded him of an Egyptian tomb. He wondered how anyone could work in such a creepy time capsule.

Her workspace looked more like a museum than a place to conduct business. The only normal item on her desk was a picture frame. Jake picked it up, observing the smiling couple. The woman in the photograph was the spitting image of Dr. Gray, or she would be if the witch doctor ever smiled. "This your sister?"

Dr. Gray snatched the frame out of his hands, placing it face down on her desk. "It's none of your business."

"Okay ..." Her reaction was as strange as her field of study. Jake's training told him she was hiding something, but he wasn't going to make his job any easier by questioning her. Resisting a shiver from the cool, dry air circulating through the room, he returned his focus to his mission. "I can get you up to speed on the investigation."

"Now?"

"Yes. Is that a problem?" he asked, trying to feign patience. Jake liked a challenge, but not more than he liked putting criminals behind bars. He never understood it when others didn't share that same sense of duty.

"Actually, yes," Dr. Gray replied with annoyance. "I'm in the middle of a noteworthy Nordic discovery that could help link modern shamanic contexts."

"That's what's so great about history, Doc. It'll be there tomorrow." Jake was momentarily entertained by his own sarcasm, but Dr. Gray was not. The way she crossed her arms indicated she didn't share his humor—or maybe any sense of humor. "Look, all I'm trying to point out is that some old Viking scribbles can take a backseat to the warm bodies I'm dealing with."

Dr. Gray drew in an offended breath. Jake could tell she was gearing up for an argument, but he knew the best offense was a good defense. "Listen, Doc, I don't want to be here any more than you want me here, but I have six victims and a feeling there will be more. Help me get a lead on the Romeo and Juliet Killer, then I'll be out of your hair, and you can go back to doing whatever it is you do here."

The woman's dark eyes widened, showing her first hint of interest. "Your case is Shakespearean? That's fascinating, but you might be better off contacting one of my colleagues in the Elizabethan literature department. My area of expertise is in Occult History and Ritualistic Artifacts."

"Trust me. I'm aware."

She crossed her arms again. "What's that supposed to mean?"

Jake dropped all pretenses. "It means dragging you out of the library wasn't my idea. I'm just following orders to have you assist me on this investigation."

"I still don't see how I can help you."

Jake stood. "Once you see the crime scene, you'll understand."

"Crime scene?" Genuine fear flashed across her features. "I don't go to crime scenes. I'm a historian. I study artifacts and rituals."

"Well, today's your lucky day. Someone's been bringing your satanic rituals to life." He tossed a case file onto her cluttered desk.

Dr. Gray rushed to her desk, but not to look at documents in the folder. She seemed much more concerned about protecting her precious books that were making a home there.

Was Cramer out of his mind? Working with this woman wasn't a viable option, and Jake was done wasting time.

"Well, if you change your mind, you know where to find me. That is if you care at all about helping the living."

4

"It's not going to work, Cramer," Jake yelled into the speaker as he fought the endless Pennsylvania Avenue traffic. "The witch doctor was just another dead end, so feel free to pass that on to whatever genius set up that waste of time."

"Relax, Shep. She'll come around."

"I'm not so sure."

"Did you leave a copy of the case file with her?"

"I didn't have much choice considering she refused to come to the crime scene."

"She's consulted on other cases for us before."

"It certainly didn't seem like it."

Cramer sounded like he was holding in laughter on the other end of the call. "Let's just say Dr. Gray has a reputation for doing things her own way, but I assure you, her input will be invaluable to this case."

"If you say so."

"I do. Get some rest, son. We'll regroup at o-six-hundred."

Jake disconnected the Bluetooth call, trying to ignore the flare of anger his boss's fatherly comment triggered. He respected Cramer, but there was only one man who'd earned the right to call him son, and that was his uncle.

When Jake's biological father refused to take responsibility for the result of his off-base extracurriculars, Jake's Uncle Wade took over. Master Sergeant Wade Shepard helped raise Jake in his early years, when Jake's mother was too shattered by heartbreak to do so. Jake counted himself lucky that her big brother Wade stepped up. It had formed an unbreakable bond between the two men—one that continued to this day.

Guilt stabbed Jake as he realized how long it'd been since he was home. But ever since he'd returned from his last tour, Nevada didn't feel like home. How could it when his unit had returned one man short?

Pushing the painful memories aside, Jake switched lanes and headed toward his favorite outlet for the anger building beneath his skin—the shooting range.

FRESHLY SHOWERED, Jake toweled off and padded barefoot through his empty apartment. At the wet bar, he poured himself a glass of bourbon. He hadn't bothered turning on the lights or dressing. Walking around naked was one of the perks of living in his own private bachelor pad.

He stood in front of his floor to ceiling windows, enjoying his eagle eye view of the National Mall. No matter how many times he saw it, DC at night took his breath away. Especially from the vantage point of his high-rise apartment.

For a rare moment, he allowed himself to study his reflection in the glass. Not just the definition of the muscles a lifetime of military service had sculpted or the way the remaining beads of water glistened on his tan skin, but he let his eyes travel over the damaged flesh his bad choices had left behind.

His scars were many, depicting a roadmap of his life. The problem was, there were just as many scars buried deep below the surface, waiting to detonate like an IED on anyone who got too close.

Deep down, Jake knew that was why he was keeping his distance from home. He didn't want to unleash his demons on Wade or his mother. They'd raised him to be a better man than he was right now. That's why he didn't plan on going back until he got his head right.

It was a long road back to the man they remembered. Jake had been walking a new path for four years since he left the service. But he still had a long way to go.

Pulling himself from his inner darkness, Jake took his first sip of bourbon, savoring the warmth that spread through him. It instantly eased his mind. He grinned faintly as he heard his uncle's voice in his head. *There's nothing quite as divine as a bottle of bourbon. That's why it's called spirits.*

Wade had taught Jake to drink his bourbon neat, *Like a real man.*

Thinking about Wade tugged at the guilt Jake had just spent hours trying to bury. He quelled it with another sip of bourbon. A few hours at the shooting range, then his home gym hadn't been enough to rid him of all his demons. But his anger had at least subsided enough to allow him to think clearly again.

As he sipped his bourbon, Jake's thoughts drifted back to the murder investigation, and of course the infuriating witch doctor, whom he couldn't seem to get out of his mind.

She was gorgeous and no doubt a genius in her field, but in his opinion, working with her wasn't worth the hassle. Which brought Jake to two important conclusions. Working this case with someone as attractive and frustrating as Dana Gray was a recipe for disaster. Ergo, working the case alone was the only solution.

Now he just had to convince Cramer of that.

5

Dana couldn't help herself. The folder was sitting on her desk, tormenting her curiosity. Of course, that's probably why the obnoxious FBI agent left it there. Claire had been right. The man was conventionally attractive, but in Dana's opinion, he was about as appealing as the idea of curling up with a slab of granite.

Agent Shepard carried himself in a cold, chiseled sort of way. He seemed like the type who enjoyed tormenting people. And with those good looks of his, he was probably used to getting what he wanted. But Dana wasn't about to give him the satisfaction. Between his rude comments about her work and his superiority complex, she had half a mind to ignore the folder just on principle.

There was little she hated more than being talked down to about the importance of her work. Yes, she studied the mystic rituals of the past. But societies that ignored the mistakes of their past were doomed to repeat them and lose any hope at a thriving future. By researching why certain occult rituals and artifacts were believed to hold power or value, she was uncovering key subcultures that still exist in current civilizations.

In today's society, these practices didn't go by archaic names like witchcraft, voodoo or alchemy anymore. Now they identified as cults, sects and extremist religious groups. All were real-world issues that her studies could help shed light onto—light the world desperately needed if world news headlines were to be believed.

It wasn't completely unheard of for specialists like herself to cooperate with police or government officials. Findings in her field helped gain a better understanding of groups like the one involved in the Waco Siege and structured a path of rehabilitation for those who were misinformed or inducted into such practices against their will.

Dana had consulted on findings for the FBI before, but never on an active case. She was usually called in after the fact whenever strange artifacts were discovered. Her most memorable had been a case involving a Russian man who attempted to assassinate a congressman. After his conviction, she was granted access to his apartment. It was full of priceless Russian artifacts. She'd spent months examining the findings and comparing them to the Slavic and Baltic artifacts the Smithsonian had access to.

In that case, she'd been called in to authenticate the artifacts since the man had claimed he was a Russian spy. And though his belongings were legitimate Russian relics, it was discovered the suspect was little more than a fervent collector diagnosed with paranoid schizophrenia. The man would now spend the rest of his days at a secure facility for the criminally insane.

Dana carefully closed the book she'd been studying and pushed her readers into her hair. She removed her gloves and rubbed her eyes before putting on her regular glasses again. Despite her best intentions, she was too distracted to get any real work done on the Nordic text she was deciphering. She'd read and re-read the same page a dozen times, unable to keep Agent Shepard and his words at bay.

That is, if you care at all about helping the living.

Of course she did. Not that he had any clue, but that's how she ended up in this field. Dana knew better than most that studying the dead was a way to serve the living.

Her eyes automatically lifted to the framed photo on the corner of her desk. The one the arrogant agent had rudely manhandled. It was one of the few photographs she had of them. Growing up, her family didn't have a lot of money. Photographs were a luxury they could rarely afford.

After Agent Shepard left, Dana returned the frame to its rightful spot. She'd grown used to the way the smiling faces of her parents haunted her, a constant reminder of the importance of her work. It had been their deaths that had set her on this path, and through her research she believed she was honoring them.

Sighing, she reached for the FBI case file. Inhaling deeply, she prepared herself to open it, knowing that her parents would want her to do what she could to help. Just because she'd yet to solve their murders didn't absolve her of the obligation to help others.

Tracing her finger along the edge of the green folder, she flipped it open, inhaling sharply at the crime scene photograph staring back at her. Despite her field of study, Dana had never been the type to believe in destiny, but she found it difficult to ignore that her life's trajectory had been preparing her for this very moment.

She knew she was staring at two unknown victims, but it was her parents' lifeless faces that she saw lying in the twin beds. And the pentagram sketched on the floor ... it was the very thing that had haunted her dreams since she was thirteen years old.

Overwhelmed with emotion and sudden nausea, Dana shoved back from the desk, stumbling to her feet.

"Dr. Gray? Are you all right?"

Dana whirled to see her intern in the doorway. *How long had she been standing there?* She quickly moved back to her desk to close the folder. "Claire, what can I do for you?"

"Nothing, I just wanted to let you know I was done for the day unless you needed me."

Dana glanced at her watch, surprised by the time. "No, that'll be all. You can go home."

"Do you want to walk out with me?" Claire asked. "I don't mind waiting."

Dana shook her head. "I have a bit more to do."

"It's late," Claire replied, concern in the younger woman's voice.

"Time is but a window." The *Ghostbusters* quote was out of Dana's mouth before she could stop herself. She was a closet junkie for cult classic fantasy films. Blushing at Claire's obvious confusion, Dana sat back at her desk to busy herself. "I'll be fine. Have a good night, Claire."

"You too, Dr. Gray."

Dana looked up when she didn't hear Claire retreat. "Is there something else?"

"Well, I was just wondering if you were going to help Agent Shepard."

"I haven't decided yet." That was a lie. The moment Dana saw the crime scene photographs she knew she couldn't turn away from this case. But saying it out loud brought back emotions that were too raw. She preferred to lie to herself just a little bit longer.

She'd face the truth tomorrow.

6

THE BRIGHT LIGHT POURING IN FROM THE EXCESSIVE NUMBER OF WINDOWS in the J. Edgar Hoover Building was making Dana's headache worse. She should've taken Claire's advice and left the library at a decent hour last night. But the dark, quiet atmosphere of her subterranean office seemed to exist in a world that time and light couldn't penetrate, lulling her into an endless cradle of research.

She hadn't gone home last night. And although she considered her research library at the Smithsonian a second home, it lacked certain creature comforts. Namely, her bed and steam shower. Thankfully, she kept a change of clothes at the office so she didn't look wrinkled on top of exhausted.

Dana hadn't meant to spend the night in the library, but time slipped away as she scoured every inch of the FBI case file. She must've fallen asleep at her desk on her third pass through.

Right now, Dana found herself missing her safe, dark world in the belly of the Smithsonian Library. There she was queen of her domain. Here she felt like a patient, being shuffled from one waiting room to the next. For all his guarantees, Agent Shepard was not as easy to locate as he'd promised.

Dana had been in the FBI building for over an hour, and she was still being promised that her time was valuable.

Standing, she gathered her things and began walking up to the receptionist when she heard Agent Shepard's deep voice echo down the empty corridor. "I was wondering when you'd turn up. Took you long enough."

Dana's teeth gritted in annoyance. "Me? I'm the one who's been waiting!"

He had the nerve to smirk. "Maybe you're not the only witch doctor I'm consulting with."

"Oh really?" Her ego got the better of her. "Did your other consultant identify the type of poison used in this case? Because I did."

Agent Shepard crossed his arms. "Not possible. We don't have the tox screen back yet."

"You don't need a tox screen. You have me." Dana marched forward and thrust her findings at him.

He took the folder and opened it, leafing through her notes. From the way he was squinting, she knew he might as well be looking at hieroglyphics. Sighing, she invaded his space, getting a whiff of his spicy aftershave. She didn't let the alluring scent of sandalwood distract her as she peered over the paperwork with him. "It's atropa belladonna. Also known as nightshade; a deadly perennial herbaceous plant. Translation, it won't show up on your tox screen."

"Why not?"

"Well, it only stays in your system for a few hours, but mostly because it's an alkaloid, not a toxin that's traditionally on a drug panel."

"How do you know that?"

Dana fought her urge to roll her eyes. She wasn't the one on trial here. She exhaled. "Because it's been used as a poison since at least the fourth century BC in Egyptian and Roman rituals. It then moved into Islamic Empires before finding its way to Europe. If you're interested, I can recommend a few pagan manuscripts that detail the many uses of nightshade." Agent Shepard blinked at her; his clueless expression almost endearing. "Stop me if I'm going too fast."

"All right, I get it. You know your stuff. I don't need a history lesson, just the CliffsNotes that pertain to our case."

"Our case?"

"You're here, aren't you?"

Dana ignored his sarcasm. She'd earned it with her boastful tête-a-tète. But she couldn't help it. Shepard's arrogance got under her skin. Exhaling, she decided the best course of action was to table their differences. It was the only way she was going to get answers. And she desperately wanted them. "Nightshade is a nearly untraceable drug used in all manner of pagan rituals. It can cause a myriad of deadly side effects like delirium, hallucination, paralysis and tachycardia."

"We're still waiting to hear about the current scene, but heart attack was COD on the first four vics."

"That makes sense. It can render the body immobile while having the complete opposite effect on the heart."

"Why would this be used in a ritual?"

"Some cultures believed a few drops in the eyes would not only make you more attractive by dilating one's pupils, but it could also grant the gift of sight."

"So what happened? Some freaky witches took a bad trip and figured out they could use their flower power to murder people?"

"I wouldn't put it quite that crudely, but yes. Only nightshade hasn't been used in a murder on record in the US in nineteen years."

Agent Shepard's icy gaze narrowed. "That's specific."

Dana ignored his accusatory look. "I wrote my dissertation on it."

"What made you choose that for a thesis?"

Feeling exposed she changed the subject. "Is there somewhere we can go to discuss this further?"

"Actually, I was on my way to the crime scene. I could use another set of eyes."

Dana balked. "I don't think I'm ready for that."

She hated how weak her voice came out. Everything about this case made her feel vulnerable. She knew if she agreed to work with the FBI, her connection to the case would come out. But she didn't know Agent Shepard, and she certainly didn't trust him.

He took a step closer, his demeanor shifting as he dropped the stony-faced government agent act just long enough to let a sliver of compassion slip out. "I'm sorry. I know visiting a crime scene isn't easy. I won't push you. But if you're right about this drug—"

"I am," she interrupted.

A ghost of a smile played on his lips. "Then I think you could be the key to solving this case and giving the victims' families the closure they deserve."

Dana's heart froze in her chest. For a moment she could do nothing but stare at Agent Shepard, wondering just how much he knew about her, because his words rang true. They were the exact thing to say to get her to agree to committing herself to this path, no matter what it revealed about the secrets she kept locked away.

7

JAKE CHEWED THE INSIDE OF HIS CHEEK, A BAD HABIT HE'D DEVELOPED when he felt skeptical. He heard his uncle's voice as clear as day in his head. *You'll never beat me at poker with a tell like that.*

Considering Jake's current position with the FBI required a poker face at all times, it was something he worked on. It's why he'd taken up a new habit. Unwrapping a piece of cinnamon gum, Jake popped it into his mouth to mask his worrisome chewing.

Dr. Dana Gray sat across from him in his office looking as out of place as he had in her cave-like library lair. She sat ramrod straight in the chair on the opposite side of his desk, her thumb absently scraping the skin on the back of her tightly clasped hands. Her thick, dark hair was down today. It hung in lazy waves past her shoulders. Dr. Gray's hair was the only relaxed thing about her—another thing that made Jake uneasy.

What did she have to be so nervous about?

He wasn't satisfied with her vague answers about her choice of dissertation or her absolute certainty that the tox screen would validate her claims about the nightshade. She was holding something back from him. The question was, why?

But that would have to wait. The fact was, the vexing brunette was giving him his first lead in this case, and he couldn't ignore it.

"Well, if what you've outlined here is true, it seems there's only one thing left to do," Jake said.

Dr. Gray leaned forward. "What's that?"

"Make it official." Jake opened his desk drawer and pulled out a temporary access card, placing it on the desk in front of Dr. Gray. "Welcome to the FBI."

"W-what?"

He tried to hide his amusement at her startled, doe-like eyes. "Relax. It's just a temporary access card. You'll need it to get clearance to this level of the building and it'll grant you access to the case files. Make sure you wear it when we visit the crime scene."

"*If* I visit the crime scene," she clarified.

"I realize you're stepping into uncharted territory here, but if we're going to work together, I need you to commit fully. That's the only way this type of partnership is going to work."

"A partnership goes both ways," she warned.

Jake stood and stepped around his desk. "I'm aware of that."

Dana stood, too. She was tall for a woman, but his muscular frame still dwarfed hers, though she didn't seem intimidated.

"Fine," she said. "I'm in."

Jake picked up the plastic access card and clipped it to the lapel of her blazer, hoping he wouldn't come to regret inviting her weird world of the occult into his orderly one. "Welcome aboard, Doc."

8

A WAVE OF DIZZINESS CRASHED OVER DANA AS SHE FOLLOWED AGENT Shepard down the hotel corridor. It felt like the walls were closing in on her. Trying to calibrate her breathing, she looked down at the floor, concentrating on putting one foot in front of the other, but all she could focus on was the carpet pattern. It brought the images from the case file crashing back.

She knew there was no sense in trying to block it out. In a few minutes, they'd be in the very room where it happened. The same room where the killer had stood. Bile burned the back of her throat and her eyes watered, but she forced herself to keep it together. Agent Shepard was right. The victims' families deserved closure. Never having gotten that herself, she knew what a gift it could be. She was determined to do her best to make that happen for these suffering families.

Steeling her nerves, she stopped outside the hotel room door and took a deep breath. Her parents' unexpected death had taken so much from her. She refused to let it have more power over her by being too weak to do this job. Exhaling, Dana walked into the room, ready to examine the first lead in the mystery she'd dedicated her life to solving.

She knew what she'd find—police tape, print rosin, evidence

markers—but still, she wasn't prepared for how heavy her heart would feel actually being in the space. It was like a stone in her chest, making it impossible for her to pull air into her lungs. The stillness of the room was suffocating, almost like the essence of the violence that had taken place here lingered, waiting to attach onto the next unsuspecting victim.

With a hand over her mouth, Dana did her best to breathe through her sleeve. She should've brought a mask. The chemical odor from the forensic team mixed with the smell death left behind was making her sick. On the drive over, Shepard had explicitly warned her to go into the hall if she thought she was going to be ill so she wouldn't contaminate the scene.

"Remind me why we're here again?" Dana asked, hoping that talking would distract her from her queasiness.

"I like to walk in the shoes of the killer. Sometimes it helps uncover more clues."

Agent Shepard pulled the folder from under his arm and spread photos of the victims on each bed, making it impossible for Dana not to imagine what their last moments must've been like. The woman was blonde and petite. The man was broad shouldered and wore glasses. Dana's father wore glasses. Was that part of the killer's MO?

Dana pushed her parents from her thoughts. The similarities in their murder and this current one were undeniable, but Dana had been searching for their killer for nineteen years with no luck. Maybe focusing on this case would finally give her the answers she'd been trying to find. Tying her hair back tighter, she thought, *what have I got to lose?*

Focusing on the photos on each bed, Dana tried to do what Shepard said and put herself in the shoes of the killer. But no matter how hard she tried, her mind slipped into the role of the victim. It's not that she saw herself that way—far from it actually—but it was hard not to empathize with them and what they must've gone through.

She wondered if they'd known what was coming when they entered this room? Had they suffered? Had her parents?

Her head swam with lifeless faces, the victims' features melting into her parents' until she didn't know where one ended and the other began. This wasn't helping. Coming here had been a mistake. The only things Dana ascertained from the crime scene were horrible new images to haunt her sleepless nights.

Agent Shepard's voice pierced her nightmare. "Thanks to the hotel cameras we have a time stamp of when the victims entered the room, which was shortly after eight pm. We're estimating TOD between eight and nine."

"TOD?"

"Time of death," he explained without looking up from the folder. "That means our unsub," his gaze left the folder this time. "Unsub basically means unknown suspect."

"I know that," she snapped. "I've seen CSI."

Shepard shut his folder. "Fantastic! Well I guess my job is done here."

This time Dana couldn't stop her eyes from rolling. She wanted to wipe the smug look off his face, but she wanted answers more. "Please continue."

Shepard didn't even try to hide his cocky smirk as he opened the folder again. "Based on TOD, the unsub didn't waste any time. There's no forced entry at this crime scene or any of the others. No one caught on the security footage entering the room with the vics. No sexual assault or mutilation. The empty poison vials and pentagram are his signature. Letting us know he used some type of unknown substance to kill them."

"And you tested the vials for traces of poison?"

"Of course. But they were bone dry. Free of prints and never used for anything other than to taunt us. I even traced them to the dozens of big box stores that carry them in the tri-state area which was a big fat dead end." Shepard tucked his folder under his arm. "The only thing we have out of the ordinary is this."

He pointed to the pentagram drawn on the carpet, but Dana was already looking at it. It was hard to ignore. She hadn't been able to tear her eyes away from it for very long since entering the room. It was identical to the one she'd burned into her memory save one thing. All the points weren't filled in. Meaning this killer wasn't finished.

A clammy wave of sweat broke out on her neck as Dana felt the world go fuzzy around the edges. She turned to leave the room before she broke the one rule Shepard had implicitly warned her not to. But she'd only taken two steps before her knees buckled.

She opened her mouth to cry out, but her throat was so dry nothing came out. Gasping, she reached for anything to keep her from falling. She wasn't sure she could handle it if she ended up on the floor just like the victims probably had. But her concern was premature because Agent Shepard's reactions were as fast as his witty comebacks.

The last thing Dana remembered was the scent of his cinnamon gum as Shepard's strong arms slipped around her, lifting her to safety.

IN THE HALL Dana caught her breath, sipping slowly from the water bottle Agent Shepard offered her. His hand was still on the small of her back, like he expected her to black out again at any moment. She hated herself for being so weak. She hated herself even more for craving the warmth of his touch. It was spreading through her like coffee.

What had made her think she could handle this? She'd always had trouble maintaining focus in the real world. That's why she preferred the orderly and controlled environment of her research library. Outside its protective walls, there was nothing to stop the flashbacks of her parents' murder from overwhelming her. Today was proof of that.

Suddenly insecure about her ability to help, Dana felt her confidence dissolving. She swallowed, collected what was left of her pride and stood taller, breaking their connection as she turned to face Shepard. "I'm sorry. I want to help, but I can't do this."

"Hey, don't apologize. I know this isn't easy, but you're doing fine. Better than I did at my first scene."

She brushed off his comment, knowing he was just saying what he thought she needed to hear so he could get her back on the job. But she was on to him.

"You don't believe me?" He hung his head, chuckling softly. "I wish I was making it up, but I got sick at my first scene."

Dana cut her eyes at him, not in the mood to be patronized.

"I'm serious. My nickname was Yak for a whole year. Why do you think I drilled the no puking rule into your head on the drive over?"

"I saw the medals in your office. You served in the military before coming to the FBI."

"I did. Army. 101st."

"And you expect me to believe you didn't see worse during your time in the Army?"

"I did, but that was different."

"How?" she challenged.

Jake's blue eyes grew dark and distant. It was like watching a storm roll in. Dana instantly regretted her question. It obviously sent him back to a place he wasn't fond of. She was searching for a way to change the subject when he surprised her with an answer. "In war, death is inevitable, expected. But here, we're supposed to be safe. And walking into scenes like this, seeing the pointless hate people can inflict on each other ... it's not something you can be prepared for or get used to."

"How do you do it?" she asked, her voice barely a whisper.

Jake's gaze came back from that faraway place, his eyes calm again when they met hers. "I believe I'm making a difference. Setting right some wrongs."

His words hit home again and just like that, a renewed strength enveloped her. "That's what I want to do."

"I can see that." Jake's gaze softened. "It's okay to take your time. You'll know when you're ready to go back in."

She nodded. "I'm ready now."

Back in the hotel room, Dana took in the scene with a new determination. She'd removed her emotions, compartmentalizing the painful memories of her parents and even the unknown victims. She was here to do what she did best, research and analyze.

"Two of the points aren't filled in."

Agent Shepard scratched his head. "What?"

"The pentagram. Only three of the five points are filled in."

"Okay . . ." Shepard drawled.

"It means the unsub's not done."

"Excuse me?"

"The pentagram is drawn in blood, correct?"

Jake nodded. "Yes, but we're not sure whose blood. Forensics confirmed it's not the victims' and they haven't gotten any hits in the system."

"It could be the killer's blood."

"And why do you say that?"

"This scene is reminiscent of sacrificial rituals for passage to the afterlife. In these types of sacrifices, the individual conducting it offers their own blood in order to gain the power granted by sacrifice. Each time a sacrifice is made, a point of the star is filled in until all five have been completed symbolizing the price has been paid in full."

"The price?"

"For passage into the afterlife."

"So, this unsub is killing innocent people to get to some imaginary afterlife?"

"There's no proof afterlife is imaginary, Agent Shepard."

He huffed his disagreement. "I'm not here to debate heaven and hell with you, Doc. But there's a flaw in your theory."

"What's that?"

"We have six victims. That negates your little satanic scheme."

"It's not a scheme. Human sacrifice has been practiced for centuries. Some cultures held tournaments, the winners earning the right to be sacrificed to the gods. The Inca sacrificed children, pampering and fattening them for years to appease their gods with their offering. And in the city of Ur, human sacrifice was an event cele-brated annually, most often sacrificing pairs, lovers or mates to be exact."

The creases on either side of Agent Shepard's frown deepened. "Do I even want to know?"

"The relevance of pairs predates biblical times. Think of the Ark. 'Two by two they have come in unto Noah, unto the ark, a male and a female, as God hath commanded Noah'."

Shepard balked at the bible verse. "Whoa, whoa, whoa! Are you saying our killer is some kind of religious nut?"

"Not at all. By my estimates, we're dealing with an educated extremist with basic knowledge of law enforcement."

"That narrows it down," Agent Shepard muttered.

"It does if we can identify the drug."

"I thought you already did that?"

"Oh, I'm certain it's nightshade, but I'd still like to see a copy of the toxicology report."

"So would I, because if you're right, we're racing against the clock before this guy strikes again."

9

Although she had stumbled at the crime scene initially, Dana was proud of herself for pushing past her comfort zone. She'd been able to shed new light on the case and saw now why Agent Shepard and the FBI had turned to her for answers.

If they only knew the half of it, she thought as she used her keycard to access the staff elevator. Shepard followed her silently into the cold metal box, standing as still as a statue as they moved slowly to sub-level three. Dana used the few moments the quiet voyage allowed to separate the scene she'd witnessed today from the one she knew by heart. She'd need to compartmentalize them in her mind if she was going to be at her best.

Trying to solve the mysterious deaths of her parents led Dana to carve a career out of occult studies. It seemed it was finally paying off. The similarities she'd just examined at the crime scene today were so eerily akin to her parents' that she'd ruled out any chance of coincidence. Besides, there were no coincidences in science.

Many colleagues Dana had worked with argued that occult studies weren't a science. And from Shepard's sarcasm, it was obvious that he held little stock in its value. But Dana disagreed, and she wasn't going to stop until she proved them wrong and solved this case. *And maybe her parents' too.*

"One step at a time," she whispered to herself.

"What was that?" Shepard asked, his voice startling her.

He'd been so still she'd momentarily forgotten he was there. "It's nothing. Just a mantra I sometimes use."

Agent Shepard's keen blue eyes studied her. She felt herself warm under his scrutiny, grateful when the elevator doors slid open. She rushed out, his footsteps following behind her.

The cool atmosphere and scent of aged papyrus instantly put her at ease. Back in her element once again, Dana's mind began to clear, allowing her to process her thoughts. She bypassed her office and went straight to the stacks.

She liked to sort out problems in her head, letting them filter and rearrange until they fit together like perfectly arranged Tetris pieces. This was a learning technique she'd developed as a child, and it required utter silence—something that caused social isolation and led to ridicule by her classmates.

She remembered that time in her life—when she'd thought things like popularity were important. Losing her parents at such a young age had changed Dana's priorities. She saw the world through a clearer lens now, and she was grateful for it. Other people's opinions of her didn't matter. Only the truth did.

10

"So what are we doing here?" Jake asked as he followed Dr. Gray past the dimly lit rows of tables into an even darker row of towering bookshelves.

"Give me a moment, I need silence while I think."

He huffed a laugh. "We're certainly in the right place."

The stillness of the stacks gave him the creeps. It seemed like a crypt where books went to rot. And considering the titles that stared back at him, he wasn't that far off. *The Book of Thoth. The Mystical Qabalah. The Dark Lord. The Philosophy of Natural Magic. The Voodoo Doll Spellbook.*

Damn. He'd always heard the pen was mightier than the sword. Whoever wrote these books was determined to prove it in a sinister way.

Forcing himself to take deep breaths, Jake pushed away the pressing fact that he was deep underground. He'd always feared confined spaces. Even though this floor of the library was massive with over thirty-foot ceilings, knowing he was on a level buried underground still made the walls feel like they were closing in on him.

Popping another piece of gum into his mouth, Jake focused on keeping his mind busy. Studying Dr. Gray while she worked proved the perfect distraction from his claustrophobia.

She looked more relaxed than she'd been all day as she walked down row after row of the looming stacks, her fingers absently reaching out to stroke a spine here and there as if acknowledging an old friend. Again, Jake found himself admiring her features.

Dana Gray had a subtle kind of beauty, not bothering to accentuate it with makeup or flashy clothes, which made her even more attractive to him. Jake had never liked the Capital Hill Honeys that his brothers at the Bureau went for. He attracted plenty himself, but he knew better.

In his experience, women who laid it all out there for the taking were usually more trouble than they were worth. Besides, his days of playing rescuer to damsels in distress were behind him. Now the only rescuing he did was for his victims, giving their families the closure they needed.

Jake fought the quirk of his lips as he briefly let his mind wander inappropriately about the good doctor. He wondered if any man had ever attempted to crack her rigid exterior. Even if he still was that guy who liked to play hero, he had a feeling she wouldn't be into it. Despite what happened at the crime scene today, everything about Dr. Dana Gray screamed she could take care of herself.

She was the complete opposite of any woman Jake had ever been with. Opinionated, uptight, untrusting. He held in a snort when he realized he was describing himself. He wasn't a narcissist but still, there was something about her that drew him in. He'd always had a secret thing for glasses, but he had a feeling it was the eyes behind them that made it hard for him to look away. Jake had only ever seen that same forlorn look in one other place—his own reflection.

"Here," Dr. Gray said, turning to place a giant dusty book in his hands.

"What's this for?"

Her slender brows furrowed. "I thought you were interested in the poison used to kill the victims."

"You don't just have the answers up here?" he teased, tapping his temple.

"Of course I do. But I assumed you wanted proof."

Jake couldn't hide his grin. "That was a joke, Doc. I'm with the FBI. Proof is kind of our thing."

"Right," she noted, before giving him a disapproving look. "That book is priceless. Use both hands."

"Yes ma'am."

Dana ignored his salute and solemnly returned to business.

Jake sighed, wondering how he was supposed to forge a connection with this woman. If he had it his way, he'd be working this case solo, but if he was going to be saddled with a partner, it was important they build some kind of rapport. And that meant he needed to find something beyond his obvious attraction to her.

So far, even his sense of humor wasn't working.

Dr. Gray seemed like the type who didn't even appreciate humor, which Jake found sad. Sometimes, being able to lighten the mood was the only thing that saved him from the darkness of this job. It was a difficult thing to be surrounded by on a daily basis. If she was going to survive this investigation, she'd need something bright to hold on to.

JAKE'S ARMS were full when he followed Dr. Gray back to an empty row of tables. She flicked on a light and sat down, depositing her armful of books on the table much more delicately than Jake had.

"Careful," she warned, her voice a low library whisper.

"We're the only people in here, right?"

"My assistant is here somewhere."

"Okay ..."

"Why do you ask?"

"Just wondering why you're whispering. Afraid you're gonna wake the dead?"

Again, she ignored his humor and rolled up her sleeves. She donned a pair of white gloves and handed Jake a pair, too. "Put these on so the oils in your skin don't damage the books."

Then she dove into her research, propping open books to pages she seemed to know by heart while she babbled on about the origins of witchcraft and human sacrifice. It was obvious she was in her element here, and Jake couldn't help but admire it. There was just something sexy as hell about a confident woman.

Dr. Gray's conviction grew as she discussed the strange world of the occult as naturally as if she were reciting what she had for dinner. Jake didn't believe in such things and hearing words like black magic, pentagrams and devil worship thrown around like they were anything more than folktales was hard to swallow. But he did his best to keep an open mind even though he was almost certain this was a waste of time.

In his opinion, the likelihood that this unsub was some sort of occult fanatic was a reach. It was more probable they were dealing with a twisted individual who watched one too many horror movies.

"This is how we find him," Gray said, pointing to a disturbing illustration of a horned beast kneeling over a mutilated body.

"Well, why didn't you say we were looking for a guy with horns? I'll put out an APB right now."

Dr. Gray glanced up at him and her brown eyes narrowed. "That was a joke, right?"

Jake nodded, earning himself his first grin from the doctor. He gave her one back, unable to resist the way she came alive in the library. It was perhaps the sexiest thing about her. He quickly reminded himself he wasn't supposed to find her sexy, and occupied his mind by trying to make sense of the witchy history lesson she was babbling on about. As attractive as she was, he wasn't buying what she was selling. "I don't see how some sketchy illustration about an old witchy cult proves anything about the poison used."

"That's because you're not looking at it all together. Here ... and here ..." She pointed to the horrific drawings in the books crowding the work surface. "What do you notice in all of these illustrations?"

"That there are some fucked up people in the world, but I didn't need some decrepit old books to tell me that."

Dr. Gray shook her head and started carefully moving the books around, layering the relevant pages next to each other. "These books span centuries and cultures. They're written in different languages, but all of them are saying the same thing."

"That evil walks among us?"

Dr. Gray's solemn gaze met his and for a moment her pain reached out and touched his. "That's something we can agree on."

He nodded, struck by the fact that maybe they weren't as different as he'd first thought. But he was here for answers about a case, and he needed something factual to go on. "Listen Doc, I understand this wacky world of witchcraft is important to you, but I don't need a history lesson. I need answers that apply to the real world."

"This library is my world. It's real to me. You asked for my expertise, and this is it. I've dedicated my life to understanding these rituals. Research in this field may not appear scientific at first, but if you peel back the layers, things begin to align and can be applied to the modern world."

Looking closer, he followed her fingertip as she guided him from one morose drawing to the next, pointing out the connecting thread that was initially hidden behind the hideous celebrations of death.

Jake blinked in disbelief as he recognized the same star-shaped plant in each one. Nightshade. "Well I'll be damned. You're like the Neo of this place, aren't you?"

Dr. Gray's dark eyes lit with surprise. "I'll take that as a compliment."

Jake stifled a shocked laugh. "You've seen *The Matrix*?"

"I study the dead, Agent Shepard. That doesn't mean I am dead."

"Did you just make a joke?" he teased. When she shrugged, Jake grinned. "There might be hope for us yet."

"Because I like cult classic films?"

"Because you just proved there's an interesting human buried beneath all of your witch doctor babble." She rolled her eyes, but he pressed for more, not wanting to lose the ground he'd just gained. "What other movies do you like?"

"*Ghostbusters* is my favorite."

"Get out! Me too." *Ghostbusters* wasn't really his favorite. He was secretly an *X-Men* fan. He loved anything in the Marvel universe, mostly because he could always relate to their antiheroes. But that wasn't important. His goal was to break down Dr. Gray's walls, since she was going to be his partner for the foreseeable future. "You know, you can tell a lot about a person by the movies they like."

"Really?"

"Absolutely. There's a psychological link between our personalities and the movies that appeal to us. FBI profilers rely heavily on those kinds of connections."

Dr. Gray tilted her head, curious. "So you're going to profile me based on my movie preferences?"

"I'm not a profiler."

"Then why'd you bring it up?"

"Because it would be fun to have something in common. You have heard of fun, right?"

"You want to have fun?" Her tone was offended. "We're supposed to be solving a murder."

"I know that, but we're not going to get anywhere until we learn to work together, which is easier if we can find some common ground and start building trust."

Dr. Gray mulled the idea over for a moment. "I can do that."

"Look at that! Progress."

She frowned, and Jake worried his sarcasm was eating up the ground he'd gained when Dr. Gray spoke again. "I'm sorry I've been difficult. This case ... it's opened up old wounds."

"What do you mean?"

She shook her head, the vulnerability in her voice vanishing. "Nothing. I think being at the scene just rattled me more than I expected."

"If you weren't rattled, I'd be concerned."

She offered him a tight smile. "I'm going to do everything I can to help you solve this case."

"Glad to hear it." Jake returned her smile, and for the first time he felt like he might have actually found solid ground with the incredibly gifted doctor. "I'll make you a deal. Solve this case and we'll have a *Ghostbusters* movie marathon."

Grinning, she pointed back to the drawing in the book closest to her. "Then we'd better prove that nightshade is what killed the victims."

11

"Alkaloid toxins are derived from Atropa belladonna, also known as nightshade. The plant was prevalent on multiple continents dating back to the fourth century BC. Wealthy families in Europe kept it along with other medicinal plants in what they called poison gardens."

Agent Shepard frowned. "So they were like the original meth heads?"

Dana understood the reference, but the prestigious position of tending a royal poison garden was nothing like cooking meth. She decided not to burst his bubble. She could tell the surly FBI agent was doing his best to find solid footing in her "wacky world of witchcraft," as he'd called it.

To his credit, he was at least pretending to take her seriously, scribbling furiously in his notebook. They'd been at it for hours. Whether he believed in the rituals she dedicated her life to studying was irrelevant. All that mattered to her was that she was making progress on the investigation.

This was the closest Dana had ever been to uncovering another key element of her parents' murder. When they were found dead in a hotel room, bloody pentagram on the floor, empty vials in their hands, their death was ruled a suicide. But Dana knew in her heart they never would have left her by choice, and now that she was a part of Agent Shepard's nearly identical case, she was that much closer to proving it.

They'd moved to her research lab where the computers and modern electronics were housed. It was Dana's least favorite room on her floor of the library. The harsh fluorescent lights buzzed overhead, disrupting her concentration. She knew sometimes technology was a necessary evil, but she didn't enjoy it.

Shepard was hunched over a laptop, scrolling through the FBI's database he'd accessed. They were cross referencing crimes with known poisons. So far, they had no hits for nightshade, which was discouraging. But she couldn't deny this part of the investigation felt symbiotic—both of their worlds joining in such a scientific way.

"Well, I don't know what to tell you," Shepard said, staring at the 'no search results found' screen again.

Dana stared at the blinking cursor in the white box. "Did you spell it correctly?"

"I may not have a PhD, but I did pass English 101."

"Knock, knock," Claire called, interrupting their debate. "Have you been down here all day?"

"Mostly," Dana replied.

"I paged you."

Shepard snorted a laugh. "Did you say paged? You mean that thing is actually functional?"

Dana ignored him and pulled the green pager from her belt. Damn. It was dead again. She muttered her apologies to Claire. "Sorry. It's not holding a charge like it used to."

"You've heard of cell phones, right?" Shepard teased.

"It holds sentimental value," Dana snapped, tenderly tucking the pager into her blazer pocket.

Shepard held up his hands, and Dana turned back to Claire. "Did you need me for something?"

"No, I just assumed you forgot to eat again," Claire said, moving fully into the lab. "So I just ordered your usual."

She plopped her clunky black backpack onto an empty table, the metal spikes clanking loudly against the white resin tabletop. Claire pulled out a large brown paper bag with bright red lettering that Dana knew all too well. Thaiphoon made her favorite vegan kung pao dish. Just thinking about the perfect mix of savory spices was making her stomach rumble.

As usual, Claire was right. The hours had gotten away from Dana. She was too well practiced at ignoring her grumbling stomach these days. If it wasn't for Claire, Dana would probably end up living on coffee and waffles, her only daily ritual before leaving the house. Thankfully, her intern's stomach was more reliable than any alarm clock.

Dana's mouth watered as the sweet scent of jasmine rice and spicy stir fry filled the lab. She glanced at Shepard. From the way he eyed the bag, Dana wasn't the only one who'd skipped a meal.

"I'm not sure what secret agents like," Claire said, her cheeks pinking as she continued to unpack the brown bag, "so I just got you my favorite."

Agent Shepard straightened, stretching his arms over his head as he sniffed the air. "Whatever it is, I'm grateful. I'm starving."

Claire settled in her usual spot, crossing her legs in the white over-stuffed chair in the corner of the lab. The place might appear white and sterile, but to Dana, it was home. She and Claire ate all their meals in this room since Dana didn't allow food in her office with so many price-less books and artifacts around. After Claire had been hired, they'd added a cafe table and chairs, along with the overstuffed wingback where Claire liked to curl up and read.

"So, did you crack the case yet?" Claire asked, stabbing a shrimp with her chopsticks.

Dana moved to the small dining table and unwrapped her dish. "I think we may have found the source of the poison."

"Doc, we don't talk about on-going investigations," Shepard warned, taking up the empty chair across from her.

Claire paused, a chopstick hovering near her lips, and exchanged a questioning look with Dana.

Dana cleared her throat. "Claire is my research assistant, Agent Shepard. If you want me at my best, she's part of the deal." She could tell he was going to object, so she continued singing her assistant's praises. "Claire has a near eidetic memory and is better than any online resource when it comes to reciting facts or definitions. She'll be an asset to our investigation."

"Very well. I'll work on getting her clearance." Shepard's stern glance fell on Claire. "It goes without saying that everything discussed here doesn't leave this room, understood?"

Claire's already rounded shoulders slumped further, but she agreed, her voice suddenly mousy. "I can keep a secret."

Dana caught her assistant's eye, giving her an encouraging nod, to which Claire frowned. She clearly didn't approve of this new addition to their dynamic.

Claire had come to Dana two years ago. She was a Georgetown grad student getting her PhD in Egyptology. She reminded Dana of herself —an ambitious outcast in the modern world. But under Dana's guidance, the awkward twenty-something had blossomed, finding a home at the Smithsonian, just as Dana had.

It was sad to admit that the intern was the closest thing Dana had to a best friend. They ate all their meals together and could discuss theories over their fields of study—not something she could do with outsiders.

A quick glance at Agent Shepard as he dug into his sesame ginger dumplings had Dana feeling a strange twinge of excitement. There was no doubt the government man was out of his element, but he was making an effort, and that was more than any other man had ever done. But Dana didn't have time to get her feelings involved. She was already too invested in this case to put her heart on the line more than it already was.

Besides, she'd made a decision a long time ago that love was not a ritual she wanted to explore.

12

Jake held the door to the forensics lab open for Dr. Gray. He followed her inside, trying to ignore the floral scent of perfume that trailed behind her.

After spending all night in the bowels of the Smithsonian, Jake was no closer to catching the killer than he'd been before he signed on to work with the occult specialist. There was no denying they'd made progress with their partnership, but Jake still wasn't convinced he wasn't better off going it alone.

That's why they were here. Felix Raynard was the best in the Bureau. If he couldn't connect nightshade to the case, no one could. And they finally had the toxicology report to reference.

Jake led the way to Raynard's office. He may have a more socially acceptable job than Dr. Gray, but his office was even more disturbing. Averting his eyes from the jars that held pickled remains, Jake made introductions.

"Witch Doctor, meet the Alchemist."

Raynard stood, extending a pale, boney hand. "Dr. Felix Raynard," he amended, cutting his eyes at Jake. "And you are?"

"Dr. Dana Gray."

Shepard stood by for as long as he could bear, letting the two scientists compare credentials and accolades.

"Yeah, yeah. You both have big brains, I get it. Let's get to the case."

Raynard nodded. Taking his seat, he spun his chair back toward his wall of monitors. "So, Shepard tells me you think atropa belladonna is the culprit?"

Dr. Gray nodded. "I do. But we searched the FBI database last night without any success."

Raynard grinned. "And I wouldn't expect you to."

"What do you mean?" Jake asked.

"Nightshade isn't something we'd ever test for unless it was of specific interest. And even if we did, naturally occurring toxins like nightshade are notorious for not showing up on tox screens because they have such a short half-life, something your unsub probably knows," Raynard added. "If you ask me, you're looking for someone with a background in forensic toxicology or police procedures."

Dr. Gray beamed. "Exactly what I said."

Jake was doing his best to overlook her smug grin, but it wasn't easy. Not only had she been right about the poison, but her gloating smile was sexy as hell.

"So what do we do now?" she asked.

"Now we put in a request to the coroner's office for specific labs to identify the drug."

"It's a long shot," Raynard warned. "Your vics have been cold for over 48 hours, and nightshade can leave the system without a trace in as little as three hours depending on the dose."

"We at least have to request the labs."

"Even if they're useless?" Dr. Gray asked.

Jake nodded. "Chain of evidence. We have to follow procedure. There's no way I'm letting this monster off on a technicality. While we wait for labs, we can go back to my office and take a look at the archives to see if we can link any other cases using this kind of drug."

"Actually, my department at the Smithsonian has an entire section dedicated to ancient harvesting techniques of plants like nightshade.

We might have more luck tracking the lab and greenhouse equipment required to procure enough nightshade for this many poisonings."

Raynard nodded his approval. "That's where I'd start." His gaze flickered to Jake. "You finally got yourself a worthy partner. Hold on to this one."

The comment hurt more than Raynard had meant it to, but Jake was grateful for the reminder to keep Dr. Gray at arm's length. The last thing he needed was to get too close. His line of work was dangerous and no place for emotional attachment. Emotions caused distractions and distractions could be deadly. It was something he'd learned the hard way.

"Want me to drop you at the Smithsonian?" Jake asked once they were back in his SUV.

Dr. Gray slipped her seatbelt into place. "You're not coming?"

"Do you really need me to carry more dusty books around for you?"

"I thought we were partners?"

"We are, but sometimes divide and conquer is the best tactic. I need to file the lab request."

"All right. I'll look to see if anyone was researching nightshade at the library."

"I can do you one better. One call and I can have a whole team of data analysts sorting through the browsing history of everyone in the DC area."

"Yes, but if we find someone who's checked out a book about how to grow and harvest it in the date range of the crimes, we'll narrow down our suspect pool even more."

Jake couldn't deny she had a point, but it was doubtful it would be that easy. "I'll drop you at the bat cave. You can send out a signal if you find any leads."

13

Unhappy that Agent Shepard had brushed off her ideas so easily, Dana did what she did best. She went to work, throwing herself into research mode.

It wasn't easy to push her anger away. Just when she thought she and Shepard were on the same page and finally getting somewhere, the moody FBI agent was pushing her out. But he had another thing coming if he thought she was going to be edged out of this case when she was getting so close to the answers she'd spent a lifetime searching for.

The case had to reveal something about what happened to her parents all those years ago. She would accept no other alternative. Doing so would feel too much like giving up. And that was something Dana didn't do.

"If it wasn't for you, he wouldn't even have a lead to chase down," Claire quipped, helping Dana look through the library database once she'd tracked down the relevant titles.

Dana looked up, regretting sharing her frustrations about Agent Shepard with Claire. From the spots of color dotting the girl's pale cheeks, she was even more upset about the snub than Dana was.

She had a feeling Claire knew all too well what it felt like to be excluded. The black clothes, dark nail polish and heavy eyeliner made the awkward girl a target for prolonged stares and whispers. Pairing that look with cardigans and combat boots only exacerbated the situation. Not that Dana held her unique fashion statement against her. In her own way, Dana had been an outcast, too.

After her parents died, she was sent to live with her grandparents. They were sweet and meant well, but they did nothing to help Dana fit in at her fancy new school. In DC the hand-me-down treasures that she and her mother enjoyed hunting for at thrift stores didn't have the same appeal. Without the designer jeans and preppy blazers of her classmates, she was quickly exiled.

A long-forgotten memory prickled in some dark corner of her mind. A flash of an emerald green sweater, her mom's laughter, kids teasing her for wearing it too many days in a row. Tension squeezed her chest. Dana hadn't thought about things like that in years. She didn't let herself. It was hard to move forward when dwelling upon the past. But it was always there, tapping her on the shoulder, begging her to remember.

Dana looked down at the emerald green blouse she wore. It was her color. At least that's what her mother had told her years ago. Her stubborn memories resurfaced, pulling her back ... back ... back ...

Dana remembered the day vividly. It was her thirteenth birthday and her mother took her shopping at their favorite Salvation Army thrift store. A few minutes into hunting through racks of treasures, Dana's mother called her over. She positioned Dana in front of the mirror and held a deep green sweater to her chest. "Oh sweetie, it's perfect. Look, it brings out the tiny flecks of green in your brown eyes." Her mother pressed her cheek to Dana's, her eyes wrinkling in the corners as she grinned.

"You have the same green flecks in your eyes, Mom."

Her mother winked. "Then I guess green can be *our* color."

That sweater had become Dana's favorite. It was the last thing her mother bought her. After she lost her, Dana clung to the sweater like it still somehow held a piece of her mother in the threadbare fibers. She wore it almost daily. Something the kids at her new school teased her about. But Dana didn't care. The sweater was special to her because her mother had picked it out. It was one of the few things she had left that made her feel close to her.

Her mother had been wearing the same color blouse the night she died. Dana knew this thanks to the news article she'd read that leaked two photos from the crime scene. They were the only two photos Dana had ever seen. She'd tried for years to access the files without luck. She kept a photo of her parents on her desk. It was a reminder to Dana to never stop searching for the truth.

Chasing the stinging memories away, Dana focused back on the task at hand. She scrolled through page after page of the report she'd run, cross referencing books on her list checked out during the timeline that fit the crimes. So far, only one name came up. But it was on three books, all referencing nightshade.

That had to mean something. "I think I found a suspect," she whispered.

"Who?" Claire leaned over her shoulder, blinking those wide, clear blue eyes of hers at the screen.

"Anson Barnes. He checked out, *Cultivating a Sinister Species. The Poison Gardener's Handbook. Betrayed by Botanicals: a guide to growing and harvesting deadly plants.*"

"That can't be a coincidence."

Dana grinned. "You know how I feel about coincidences."

"There are no coincidences in science," Claire recited, making Dana feel like a proud professor.

14

"How are things going?"

Jake lifted his head from his desk with a jolt, surprised when a paperclip fell from his cheek. He must've dozed off while looking through reports.

Chuckling softly, Cramer walked into Jake's office. "That good, huh?"

"Actually, I think we're making progress."

Cramer's brows arched. "Oh really? So the witch doctor wasn't a waste of time?"

Jake shrugged. "She's a lot more helpful when you don't call her that."

Cramer huffed. "I'll keep that in mind."

"She may have identified the poison, but it's a waiting game now. I spoke to the coroner and ordered more tests, this time searching for a specific toxin. It's a long shot though. Apparently, it doesn't stay in the system very long. In the meantime, I have the nerd herd looking for any suspicious browser history since there's nothing to go on in CODIS."

"You got a warrant for the browser history I'm assuming?"

Jake nodded as he leaned back in his chair and yawned. "It's not easy to track down a judge at this time of night."

Cramer laughed. "It's morning, Shep. Which probably explains why you look like you've been on a base leave bender." Cramer grinned, his hand moving to his own flawless jawline. "Speaking of, keep it tight, soldier."

Jake didn't need to look at his reflection to know he needed a shower and shave, but not more than he needed some actual sleep—desk naps didn't count. He stood, saluted the old Army captain and grabbed his jacket and keys, ready to head home.

"Why don't you get some shut-eye?" Cramer suggested.

"That's the plan."

"Good. I need you to see this case through."

Jake felt his jaw tighten. "Don't I always?"

Cramer's steel gray gaze met Jake's. "I'm not talking about Ramirez. Everyone knows that wasn't your fault."

The mention of his old teammate's name hit Jake like a bolt of lightning. For a moment he heard nothing beyond the pounding of his heart and the ringing in his ears. It brought him right back there to that moment when all hell had broken loose, and he'd lost his best friend.

Cramer was wrong about one thing.It was Jake's fault, and that was precisely why he would see this case through, and all the rest that came his way. Ramirez was the better of them and for that, Jake would endlessly be repaying a life debt to the man who'd given his own to save Jake.

"Jake ..." The sound of Cramer's voice brought Jake back to the present. The concern on his boss's face was too much to bear. It was the exact reason he didn't call his family back home. They all looked at him the same way—full of pity.

Pushing past Cramer, Jake stalked toward the door, grabbing his cell phone on the way out. The beeping voicemail button caught his attention. Jake couldn't remember the last time someone actually left a voice message. His curiosity was piqued when he saw the message was from Dr. Gray. He motioned Cramer over as he hit the speaker button and pressed play.

Dr. Gray's voice was breathless with excitement. "Shepard, I think I found him. Call me back."

Grumbling, he hit the redial button, knowing this was all part of her strategy. If she'd given him the name, he could've left her out of it. She didn't seem to consider that maybe he was doing it for her own good.

She answered on the first ring. "Where have you been? I called you hours ago."

"I was tied up. You have a name for me?"

"Yes, but are you sure we can discuss it over the phone?"

"You watch too many detective movies, Doc."

He could practically hear her rolling her eyes.

"His name is Anson Barnes. He checked out three titles that fit the profile during our timeline."

Jake was back at his desk, typing the name into the system. "Got anything else for me?"

"A home address, according to his library card."

Library cards were still a thing? He kept that thought to himself. "Give it to me."

Dr. Gray rattled off the address. Jake jotted it down, put Dana on speaker, and set the phone on his desk. With a few strokes of his keyboard, Jake had Anson Barnes' profile staring back at him. "Well look at that. Our book worm has an arrest record. But it seems he doesn't live in DC anymore."

"Where is he now?" Gray asked.

"Current home address is listed as Las Vegas, Nevada."

"Vegas?" She huffed into the phone. "But that doesn't make any sense. Our system shows the books were checked out a few months ago."

"Maybe your system is wrong."

"It's not."

"How can you be sure?"

"You carefully catalog your evidence, don't you?"

He hadn't missed the clipped tone of aggravation in her voice. "Yes."

"Well, we keep track of our books with the same precision. The dates aren't incorrect."

"Point taken."

"What was Mr. Barnes arrested for?" The anticipation in her voice had returned.

"You don't want to know."

"Actually, I do."

Cramer moved behind Jake's desk to get a better look at the man's arrest record as Jake rattled it off. "A couple of B and Es, carjacking and my personal favorite, illegal possession and distribution of pornography."

Cramer's face wrinkled in disgust. "Sounds like you found yourself a real winner."

"It could explain the staged crime scenes," Jake offered.

"I don't believe the crime scenes were staged," Gray argued.

"That may be so, but we have to explore all options. Let me look into this guy and see if we can confirm his location."

"Then what?"

"Then I go knock on some doors."

"You mean *we* go knock on some doors. I want to come."

"I don't think that's a good idea," Jake warned. "Besides, it might not even come to that."

Before she could argue, he hung up the phone and looked at Cramer. "Looks like I'm going to Vegas."

"Go home and get cleaned up. I'll make sure the plane is ready for you and Dr. Gray."

Jake stopped short. "You want me to take her with me? Into the field?"

"Didn't you already do that when you took her to the crime scene?"

"That was different. Besides, she didn't do so well."

"She found evidence that led you to a suspect, didn't she?"

Thinking of how she'd almost passed out made a surge of protectiveness flash through Jake. "She's been helpful so far, but I don't think Vegas is going to be her scene. She'll be safer if she stays in the library."

"She goes with you. That's an order."

15

As the plane approached Las Vegas, Dana couldn't quell her excitement.

Despite Jake's numerous warnings, she'd gotten her hopes up that this was their guy.

At first, she'd had her doubts, but when a deeper search into Anson Barnes' most recent credit card purchases revealed suspicious activity, she couldn't deny he was a viable suspect.

Digital forensics had verified he was using illegal pass-through accounts associated with the dark web; something she knew of, but not how to navigate. To her knowledge, it attracted exclusively sinister activity, including the purchase of drugs like nightshade.

They hadn't been able to find that Barnes had made any purchases for the drug or other similar substances. That would've been too easy. But that didn't mean he hadn't.

The fact he was using such complicated methods to disguise his financial transactions meant he was hiding something.

The discovery had thrown Dana for a loop. It was hard to ignore all the evidence pointing to Anson Barnes, but she still found herself unable to believe her parents had been mixed up with the sort of crowd Barnes associated with. But how well had she really known them?

She'd been just a kid when they'd died. There could have been all sorts of things they'd kept from her.

Dana pushed her doubts away. Anson Barnes might be to blame for the current case she was working on, but she had a hard time accepting he was responsible for her parents' deaths, no matter how similar the crime scenes were.

For one thing, he was too young.

Anson Barnes was thirty-seven. That would've made him barely eighteen at the time of her parents' death. Not impossible, but unlikely. Dana flipped through his file again. Even now, he was scrawny. She found it hard to believe that he could've overpowered her father and mother. Sure, the element of surprise might've worked in his favor, but not against two people.

Her mind worked through endless scenarios of how it might've gone down. Had her mother been surprised and used as leverage against her father? Were they both poisoned somewhere other than the hotel room? Had they been the targets or just in the wrong place at the wrong time? Did the killer work alone or have help?

Questions like these were a constant for Dana, and often why she filled the majority of her time with tedious research. It was in the silent, idle spaces like these where her mind was free to flood her with horrific hypotheses about who had taken her parents from her.

She was no stranger to these morbid imaginings, but one thing had changed. Now the previously faceless assailant took the form of Anson Barnes. The problem? No matter how hard she tried, Dana couldn't make the image stick. But that's why she was on this flight to Las Vegas. To find out once and for all if Anson Barnes killed her parents.

Heart pounding with anticipation, Dana glanced over at Jake, wondering how much longer she could keep the truth from him. She'd thought about telling him why she was so invested in solving this case when they'd first boarded the private flight, but Jake had fallen asleep almost immediately, and the moment passed.

Dana couldn't help being envious that he'd taken advantage of the flight time to catch up on sleep. She hadn't had much since the FBI Agent walked into her life, but she was used to surviving on little sleep.

Besides, she was too wired to rest when answers finally felt within reach.

As the bright lights of the Las Vegas Strip approached, Dana's chest tightened with anticipation. Though her research had taken her all over the world, she'd never been to Las Vegas. She'd always wanted to go; ever since she saw the magnet on her parents' refrigerator. Her mother told her it was a souvenir from their wedding. Dana had always loved her parents' wedding story. Her mother had told it to her so many times it became as familiar as a fairytale.

Her parents met at a party. Her father had been playing guitar. When her mother saw him, their eyes locked, and it was love at first sight. They went out to get waffles at midnight and stayed up until sunrise talking. Her father dropped her mother off at home, only to show up a few hours later with an engagement ring he pawned his guitar for. He barely managed to propose before Dana's grandpa chased her father off the property. Her mother's parents opposed the marriage because they were so young. But being desperately in love, they eloped to Las Vegas rather than wait.

The tale had always reminded Dana of Romeo and Juliet. It wasn't lost on her how ironic that was, considering the name assigned to the current case she was investigating. But that was even more reason for her to believe that her parents' death had been a part of something sinister.

It always bothered her that the police had labeled their death a murder-suicide and simply shut the case. Dana just couldn't accept that her parents would have planned such an end to their epic love story. It didn't make sense. Her parents ran away to get married. They would never voluntarily end their lives. They were too much in love.

Others might argue that love made people do irrational things, but Dana chose to find beauty in the illogical. Science was full of such examples: males of the seahorse species birthing their young, an immortal species of jellyfish, snails that slept for three years at a time.

The list was endless. It was an argument Dana used often to defend occult studies. If there was so much that wasn't understood about their own world, how could people close their minds to the possibilities of a seemingly supernatural ideology?

The plane touched down, jostling Dana from her thoughts. The squeal of the brakes woke Agent Shepard from his sleep. Gone was the peaceful, calm expression that softened his features during sleep. His hardened mask of a government agent was back, pushing away any inclination Dana had to tell him about why she was really here.

16

After a short ride from the private airport, Dana followed Agent Shepard into the Las Vegas police headquarters. The bare, beige walls were a welcome change from the bright flashing lights of the Strip.

She'd always thought herself well-traveled, but nothing had prepared Dana for some of the sights she'd witnessed during the drive.

Showgirls paraded down the street in high-heels and practically nothing else, inebriated tourists drank slushy beverages from neon cups as they stumbled down the sidewalk, prostitutes waved their wares to those cruising the Strip, and people spilled out of casinos, blinking like prairie dogs at first light. All the while, the police stood by calmly monitoring the chaos.

"Are you sure they're going to be able to help us?" Dana asked Shepard as they waited to be buzzed out of the busy police station booking room. It was currently full of drunks and hookers. Dana's eyes lingered on a handcuffed man in a batman costume who'd just vomited into his lap. "They seem like they have their hands full around here."

"The FBI maintains a working relationship with local PD when in their jurisdiction."

It wasn't an answer to her question, but she knew enough about

Shepard to see he was in business mode and not in the mood to play twenty questions. Keeping her mouth shut, she followed him further into the precinct when one of the *Employees Only* doors buzzed open.

It was much quieter away from the people being booked. They were shown to a small room and told to wait for their officer liaison. Dana sat down and took the moment to get her bearings. She couldn't quite believe where she was. She didn't spend a lot of time "in the real world" as Shepard would say, but that didn't mean there wasn't a place for her here. Moments like this made her wonder what career path she might've chosen if her life had been left to follow its natural course.

"Agent Shepard, sorry to keep you waiting." A thin man strode into the room, hand extended.

"No problem at all, Sheriff Bishop. Thanks for making time for us. This is Dr. Gray. She's assisting me with this case."

Dana stood, but before she could shake Bishop's hand he turned back to Shepard, frowning. "I wasn't aware you were bringing your own forensics team."

"Oh, she's not with the FBI. Dr. Gray was called in to help with possible ties to cult activity. She's good with the witchy stuff," he added patronizingly.

"Actually, I have PhDs in Cultural Studies and Religious Philosophy," she corrected. "So I'm a little more than good at the *witchy stuff.*" Throwing a glare at Shepard, she stepped around him to shake the police chief's hand. "I'm the curator of occult rituals and artifacts at the Smithsonian. It's a pleasure to meet you."

Bishop's wide smile gleamed under the fluorescent lights. "The pleasure's all mine."

"Let's get down to business," Shepard interrupted. "We're here to investigate Anson Barnes."

Bishop nodded. "Yes, I got the briefing you sent. What do you need from us?"

"For now, I need some local manpower, backup if this guy rabbits. I want to surveil his home address, usual haunts, speak to known associates. The plan is to tail this guy in case he's working with others."

Bishop grinned. "We got you, Agent Shepard. I'll have my guys on Barnes like sweat on a whore in church."

"Perfect. When can I meet the team? I'd like to run point on the task force. We need to get started right away."

17

GLARING OUT THE WINDOW OF HIS TWENTY-EIGHTH FLOOR HOTEL window, Jake took in the busy Strip below. From so high above, the people looked like drunken ants stumbling over each other to get to the next flashy thing. With a grunt, he closed the drapes, blocking out the harsh Nevada sun.

Jake hated Vegas. It was nothing but a hedonistic paradise for gamblers and sinners. That and it was also only a stone's throw from his hometown. He'd grown up in Ellsworth, a little blip of desert town that had popped up thanks to Nellis Air Force Base. The base was only a few miles from the Strip, so of course as a rebellious teen, he and his friends would escape to Vegas to blow off some steam.

It wasn't that his memories from those times were all bad, but he shared most of them with Ramirez, and that made looking back painful. So was the fact that he was so close to home. Jake felt guilty that he hadn't reached out to his family. Shutting everyone out while he dealt with what happened to Ramirez was the only way he knew how to cope. His mother and uncle understood, but that didn't make it fair. And being this close to them now only made his guilt weigh on him more.

Jake let his mind wander to a time when this case would be over. Maybe he'd tie it up neatly right here and make a quick trip up to see his family before heading back to DC. His Uncle Wade had retired from the Air Force a few years back, but he still couldn't bring himself to move away from Nellis and the familiar comforts that came with living near a functioning military base.

Much of Nevada was designated for US military use. That's what happened when land was cheap and uninhabited. It was a fine place to serve out your base life years, but now that his uncle was a civilian, Jake wondered why he didn't move somewhere more hospitable.

He'd tried for years to get his mother and Wade to move to the Florida Keys. Jake had gone once on leave with a fellow private. The guy's brother was retired special forces and ran a fishing charter business. Crystal clear water, palm trees, ice cold beer, running Reds all day. It had been the best five days of Jake's life. Which was pretty sad, now that he thought about it.

The Keys had always been the pot of gold at the end of the rainbow to Jake. He promised himself, someday when all this was over, he'd end up there. Having his mother and Wade there would only make that dream more likely to become a reality.

But Jake didn't have time for wishful thinking at the moment. He pushed the useless thoughts from his head to focus on the task at hand. He'd settled into his hotel room, showered, and would soon rendezvous with Dr. Gray to take a ride by Anson Barnes' place.

Bishop had assembled an acceptable task force, and Jake had assigned a team to Anson's address already, but he was a hands-on kind of guy. Jake's lips tugged at the corners as another nugget of Wade's wisdom came back to him. *Consider a stone unturned unless it was your hand that did the turnin'.*

Embracing the warmth the fond memories of his uncle filled him with, Jake finished dressing in a clean shirt and tie. A quick glance at his watch told him he only had a few minutes to scarf down the room service meal he'd ordered before meeting Dr. Gray. He lifted the lid, revealing the now cold cheeseburger. Shrugging, he polished it off quickly. Jake had eaten worse in his life. To him, food was food. He'd learned being a diligent agent had its perks. Hot meals weren't one of them.

TEN MINUTES LATER, Jake was walking through the casino floor to rendezvous with Dr. Gray. The *ding-zip-whiz* of the slot machines added to his growing headache, and the pungent smell of stale cigarettes and air fresheners reminded him how useless showers were when staying at a Vegas hotel.

One pass through the casino floor and he smelled like he'd pulled an all-nighter at a strip club. And of course, the only way out was through the casino. *God forbid the House lost out on a single opportunity to snatch at your purse strings.*

Jake found Dr. Gray waiting for him at their arranged spot next to a bank of Lucky 7 slot machines. She looked like a statue in a river of neon lights as she stood rigidly amid the chaos of the casino. If Jake wasn't so tired, it would have been comical.

"Did you get anything to eat?" he asked when he approached.

"Waffles."

"Waffles?"

"It's an inside joke."

Jake wanted to ask her to elaborate, but she spoke absently as she gazed around the hotel casino like she was at the zoo.

Again, his instincts told him she shouldn't be here. He preferred to work alone, but that wasn't the only reason he hadn't wanted to bring the good doctor along. Jake didn't want to play babysitter. If she got hurt on his watch, he'd never hear the end of it. Since she was already here, he had to man up and make the best of it.

Jake popped a piece of cinnamon gum in his mouth. "All right, Doc, let's get this show on the road."

In the SUV, he turned to look at her. Gray's normally calm demeanor had evaporated in Sin City. She looked anxious as she stared out the window, chewing her nails. More guilt washed over him. He shouldn't have made that demeaning comment about her in front of Sheriff Bishop. Jake may not believe there was any truth to the hoodoo voodoo nonsense that Dr. Gray peddled, but it wasn't his job to pass his judgement to others. Especially when there was no denying that her obscure knowledge had proved valuable to this case already.

"Look, Gray. I'm sorry about what I said at headquarters. You're the reason we've gotten this far."

She blinked her dark brown eyes, looking at him like she'd just rejoined him from some faraway world. "Do you really think Anson Barnes is the killer?"

"You don't?"

The question had been rhetorical. The thin frown lines etched in Gray's ivory skin gave all the answer Jake needed, but she answered anyway. "I just don't see it."

"It was your expertise that led us to him."

"I know, but it doesn't add up. Barnes is a pornographer."

"So?"

"So, how does one make the leap from porn to murder?"

"Maybe one of his movies went too far."

Gray shook her head. "The crime scene didn't look like a low-budget film set."

Jake's lips hitched at the corners. He couldn't help himself. "You watch a lot of porn, Doc?"

"More than you'd probably expect. In the name of research, of course," she clarified.

"Of course." Jake fought the playful grin she'd almost surprised out of him. The tension broken, he asked, "All joking aside, why don't you think Barnes is our guy?"

"I have my reasons."

"Care to let me in on them?"

"Not yet."

Jake shook his head. Walls back up, they drove the rest of the way to the suspect's house in silence. Something was off. Gray had been the one who'd found Anson Barnes and insisted on coming to Vegas with him. Why was she sure they were barking up the wrong tree all of a sudden?

He didn't know what the evasive witch doctor was holding back, but he planned on finding out.

18

Tired of the silence stretching out between them, Dana spoke up. "How long do these stakeouts usually last?"

Shepard didn't take his eyes off the house. "As long as they have to."

Sighing, Dana reclined her seat. "This is a waste of time." She didn't bother to hide the aggravation from her voice, and Shepard noticed.

He turned to glare at her. "We've only been here two hours."

"Yeah, but the officers we spoke to when we got here said no one's been at Barnes' place all day. Why don't we go in and take a look around?"

"I thought you didn't think he was our guy?"

Dana sighed. "I don't, but sitting out here doing nothing won't prove that."

"I'm a federal agent. I can't knock down the door without a warrant."

"Maybe you need a warrant, but I don't."

Dana's hand was on the door handle, but Shepard was faster. "Don't even think about it," he growled, his body invading her personal space as he grabbed her door, pulling it closed. "My job is to keep you safe."

Shepard's muscular arm pressed across her chest like a sinewy seatbelt, his cologne wrapping around her even tighter. He smelled like sandalwood and fresh laundry, and his touch ... it was iron, strength, safety. In another life, she would've craved him. But Dana didn't have time to enjoy the warmth of his touch. She shoved him off of her. "No, your job is to solve this case!"

His steely gaze narrowed. "What is your deal with this case?"

"Deal? Do I really need a reason to want to put a killer behind bars? Besides, you're the one who came to me, remember?"

"Yeah, not by choice."

"That's perfectly clear." Dana huffed. "If you don't want me here, just say the word. Until then I'm here to clinically observe and offer my expertise."

Shepard laughed. "Clinical my ass. You were about to go bust down a door. I'd say you have more than a clinical interest here and if you want to continue working this case, it's time you let me in on whatever you've been hiding."

Dana's heart wedged itself in her throat. She wanted to trust him. The truth was practically clawing at her, begging to be freed. But she barely knew Jake Shepard. And what she did know didn't make her think the truth about her past would paint her in a good light.

She'd assessed that he didn't believe in the subcultures she'd dedicated her life to researching. If she told him her theory about her parents, he'd think she was just as crazy as the factions she studied. Or worse, he'd take her off the case for lacking objectivity. Truthfully, she couldn't blame him for either reaction. So, Dana chose the only option she had left—action.

She was out of the car and racing toward Barnes' front door before Shepard had a chance to stop her.

Dana had no way of knowing who or what awaited her inside, but she wasn't worried. She knew Shepard would do the cliché hero thing and follow her. Not to mention that police backup was only a call away. The move was desperate, and it would most certainly get Dana kicked off the case if it didn't work, but she couldn't sit by and do nothing. Not when she was so close to finding out if Anson Barnes was the man who had stolen her chance at a normal life.

For a few fleeting moments, nothing stood between Dana and the front door but a patch of parched lawn. But if she didn't pump her legs faster, she knew it would only take a matter of seconds for Shepard's long stride to chew up the lead she'd gained on him. She'd already heard his car door open and close, his shoes pounding pavement after her. She ignored his hissed calls for her to stop.

Dana barreled straight up the three stone steps leading to the entrance of the old ranch-style one-story. As expected, it was locked, but she wasn't going to let that stop her. Turning, she caught Jake's enraged expression as he charged toward her, yelling something that was drowned out by the sound of breaking glass.

The side light panel next to the front door shattered without nearly as much effort as Dana had expected when she drove her elbow into it. Kicking the frosted glass free, she tugged her sleeve over her hand and used it to protect her skin as she reached in and unlocked the door, slipping inside, seconds before Shepard could stop her.

19

Jake stood outside for a split second before deciding to follow Gray inside. He couldn't very well stand on a stoop and let her get herself killed. In that moment a dozen valid and legal scenarios flashed through his mind, letting him know he'd still have a job after pursuing her into the suspect's house she'd just broken into.

Bewildered, he mentally reviewed what he knew about the unpredictable doctor. There hadn't been any B and Es in her file, but she'd busted into the house like a pro. If Jake wasn't so pissed, he'd be impressed.

Pulling his Sig Sauer 9mm from his hip holster, he methodically cleared the entrance, then living room. He systematically made his way through each room until he was certain there was no threat. Satisfied, he took a moment to scope out his surroundings.

The house was sparse as far as furniture and surprisingly spotless. Just the way Jake liked it. He hated cluttered scenes. They left more room for error during search and seizure. If he had a dollar for every time he'd found a suspect in a hidey-hole, he could've retired by now.

Thankfully, Barnes' modest but meticulously clean home didn't show any of the typical signs of criminal activity. No drugs left about, no visible weapons. The only thing that drew Jake's attention was the man's impressive collection of porn, which was proudly displayed on three black bookshelves in the living room. Not entirely odd considering his profession.

The smell of lemon Lysol led Jake to the kitchen. Again, the room was spotless. Dana stood next to a dented, white refrigerator. What the hell was she doing? Looking for a snack?

"Dana," he hissed, forgoing formality. That ship had sailed the moment he followed her into a suspect's house without a warrant. "We can't be in here."

"I need proof one way or another."

"We broke in. Any evidence we obtain will be inadmissible in court."

"I broke in," she clarified. "And I found the only evidence we need."

"What's that?"

"I know why Barnes hasn't been home. He's here."

Jake moved closer, noting the flyer taped to the fridge. *ANA Awards: Party like a Porn Star at the Adult Entertainment Expo. Hard Rock Hotel.*

"Look at the dates," Gray said, pointing in case he'd missed the obvious. "That's today."

Shaking his head, Jake grabbed her by the arm and directed her back to the front door. She struggled against his hold like a petulant child.

"Let go," she snarled.

"No."

"Where are we going?"

"Shopping."

"What?" Dr. Gray finally stopped dragging her feet. "Shopping?"

"You heard me."

She blinked up at Jake, those untrusting brown eyes scrutinizing him. "Why?"

"Because we've got a date with Anson Barnes at the Hard Rock, and I have a feeling we're not going to blend in dressed like a couple of feds."

"I'm not a fed," she snapped. "And I know how to blend in."

"Please. You have librarian written all over you."

Gray crossed her arms. "Excuse me?"

Jake couldn't help getting under her skin, and frankly she deserved it after the stunt she just pulled. He let his gaze travel the length of her, from her boring black shoes to her tweed blazer, to the glasses tangled in her messy bun. "The only way this look could scream book mouse any louder is if you traded those sad things in for orthopedics," he said, toeing her shoe with his own polished oxfords.

Dana's cheeks flushed a satisfying scarlet as her full lips parted into an incredulous O. "There is nothing wrong with the way I dress."

Jake grinned as he took her arm again. "I'm betting every shop on the Strip would beg to differ. Come on. We've got a party to attend."

BISHOP'S deep voice boomed through the phone. "I'll take care of it, Shopard."

"With discretion," Jake cautioned.

"Of course."

Jake breathed a sigh of relief. "Thanks, Bishop. I owe you one."

"Don't mention it. But you might want to keep that doctor of yours on a shorter leash."

"Tell me about it," Jake grumbled.

Hanging up the phone, Jake stood up and paced. Dana was taking forever in the dressing room. He'd picked out his ridiculous apparel, checked out and changed already. But jeans and a cheesy t-shirt didn't really require a fitting or a shopping assistant.

The saleswoman's eyes had lit up when Jake said he wanted to buy his "girlfriend" a new look. She'd immediately whisked Dana away to the dressing rooms.

That seemed like ages ago.

Jake was half tempted to show the saleswoman his badge to speed up the process, but he knew better than to raise unnecessary suspicion. It was better the woman thought Jake and Dana were some kinky couple here on an indulgent vacation. Smashing their way into Barnes' house was bad enough. Thankfully, Bishop agreed to call in a favor and have the glass panel repaired. With any luck, Barnes would never know what happened.

Jake checked his watch and groaned. He paced for another five minutes before impatience took over. Wanting to stay undercover, he tried out a pet name that felt foreign on his tongue. "Babe, we've gotta get going."

When Gray didn't reply right away, Jake had visions of her slipping out the back with an armful of pleather lingerie to add to her Vegas crime spree. He was about to bust into the dressing room when the saleswoman called back. "She's almost ready."

A moment later, the red curtains parted, and Jake's jaw dropped.

The transformation was as shocking as Dana's choice of outfit.

He knew it wasn't possible, but it felt like she'd chosen this look on purpose. The black leather jumpsuit fit her like a second skin, hugging the curves she normally kept buried under her sensible blazers and slacks. Her wavy brown locks tumbled loosely down her back, taking on an almost reddish hue thanks to the tawdry red lighting of the scandalous adult store.

The skintight jumpsuit combined with Dana's sultry hair made the comparison uncanny. If Jake didn't know better, he'd think he was staring at Black Widow—the Scar-Jo version, which was his ultimate fantasy.

"Well, what do you think?" the pushy saleswoman asked, giving Dana a little shove out of the dressing room. She nearly stumbled on her stilettos. Jake was so mesmerized by Dana's transformation that his response was slightly delayed as he rushed forward to catch her.

He caught her arms, and she steadied herself, her cheeks as red as the lights in the store. "You don't have to say it, I know I look ridiculous," Dana muttered for only him to hear.

Jake swallowed the inappropriate feelings rushing to the surface with Dana's warm body so close to his. "That's not what I was going to say."

Dana raised her eyebrows in challenge. "Really? Then why were you speechless when she opened the curtains?"

"You just surprised me."

"You mean you were surprised I could look like anything other than a librarian?"

Jake smirked, playfully cocking his head as he took a step back and scratched his chin.

Worry sketched Dana's features. "What?"

"Nothing, it's just now you look like a superhero librarian."

Dana swatted at him, stumbling again.

Jake reached out to steady her. "Are you going to be able to walk in those things?"

Dana's eyes danced with mischief. "Look at it this way. At least I'll be easier to catch the next time I try to outrun you."

"Very funny." He looked back at the saleswoman. "We'll take it."

She clapped her hands gleefully. "Wonderful. I'll ring you right up."

"Sorry," Dana whispered as they approached the register.

"About what?"

"This was the most expensive thing she showed me, but it was the only outfit that wasn't made of dental floss and feathers."

Jake did his best to stop his visceral reaction to the image her words conjured in his mind. "It's fine." He cleared his throat and handed over his credit card.

Out on the street, Jake did his best to shield Dana from the stares she was attracting, but it was useless. Even on the Strip, she stood out like a beacon of untamed beauty, luring in all the fools who thought they might stand a chance. And Jake felt like the biggest fool of them all for not truly seeing her until right now.

It wasn't the sexy outfit or the reminder of his boyhood fantasy, but her courage that drew him in. It'd been buried before, but Dana had somehow shed some of her defenses when she left her safe little librarian uniform behind. What remained was a fearless and formidable woman; one who Jake was lucky to have by his side, even if it was only for the time being.

"What's wrong?" Dana asked after he rushed her into the SUV.

"Nothing. Let's go catch a bad guy. And this time, you follow my lead."

20

If Dana thought the Strip was the worst Vegas had to offer, she had been sorely mistaken. The Adult Entertainment Expo was a sex addict's dream come true. It wasn't that Dana was naïve. She'd had healthy sexual relationships and her research into occult rituals often led to the exploration of sexual culture, but the things she saw on display at the expo weren't healthy. In fact, most were celebrating cruel fetishes and demeaning societal stereotypes.

"Try to keep your mouth closed." Shepard teased. "I don't want anyone mistaking you for a blow-up doll."

She glared at him. The only reason she didn't comment on his rude joke was because she knew he was using his sarcasm as a coping mechanism. From the stiff set of his shoulders and hardened jaw, she knew he was as uncomfortable as she was. She wanted to tell him he'd gotten off easy. At least he was still in his own shoes.

Shepard only had to trade in his suit for jeans and a well-fitting t-shirt that accentuated his superior upper body strength. She'd seen more than a few women working the expo floor take notice, before turning envious eyes on her.

Shepard's arm was securely fastened around Dana's waist, partly to keep her from tripping on her ridiculous heels, partly to sell their cover that they were just another couple here to enjoy the expo. Dana took it all in as they made their way through the crowd of patrons that meandered from booth to booth. People stopped to take photos with models or peruse the colorful assortment of sex toys and videos available for purchase. If it wasn't for the way everyone was dressed, or rather undressed, the whole scene reminded Dana of a craft fair or straw market.

As she did her best to blend in and not fall on her face, Shepard went to work, discreetly showing a photo of Barnes on his phone to see if anyone had seen him. So far, no luck.

They continued their lap around the expo floor. Dana flinched when Shepard tightened his hold around her waist as a man with a snake approached. The albino boa constrictor curled around the large man's neck, lazily tasting the air with its tongue. Dana didn't mind the snake as much as the man stroking it. His gaze was sinister and pointed straight at her. She didn't like the way he was looking at her, but the forceful way Shepard was steering her away was even more irritating.

Dana was no shrinking violet. She didn't need anyone's protection. Shepard should've surmised as much after she'd broken into Barnes' house, but based on the death grip he had on her, he hadn't learned his lesson. She was about to tell him she had enough taekwondo training to take care of any creep in this place when the burly snake charmer stepped into their path.

He pulled a hot pink pamphlet from the satchel around his wide waist and offered it to Dana. "Hey gorgeous, looking for representation?"

"She's good," Shepard answered, starting to steer Dana away.

She stood her ground, smiling at the man and taking the pamphlet. She even threw him a wink before letting Shepard guide her away.

"What the hell was that?" he growled when they were out of earshot.

"You're the one who said we needed to play the part. What happened to every person is an opportunity?"

"Yeah, just not guys with snakes, okay?"

Shepard shivered, making her grin. "You're afraid of snakes?"

"Some fears are healthy," he argued. She was about to tease him further when something on the pamphlet caught her eye. "Hey, look at this. Isn't this the name of one of the film companies Barnes was caught pirating?"

"You're right." Shepard pointed to the booth number. "Let's go check it out."

As they rounded the corner and the booth came into view, so did Anson Barnes. Dana's heart skipped a beat. "Holy shit! That's him."

"Stay here," Shepard ordered.

"Not a chance."

Shepard's jaw tightened with objection, but Dana cut him off. "You're not leaving me behind. Besides, you'll look less intimidating if you approach Barnes with me on your arm. And I have the pamphlet that directed us to his booth," she said, waving the pink paper under Jake's nose.

Swearing under his breath, he conceded. "Fine, but we're doing this my way. I do the talking."

They approached the booth, Dana doing her best to remember how to breathe. For once, she was glad she had someone by her side to take the lead. This could be it. The moment she got the answers she'd spent her life searching for. Would she look into this man's eyes and find the closure she craved? Or would this be another dead end?

Jake didn't waste any time. He approached the short, balding man standing behind a table filled with DVDs. "Anson Barnes?"

The man nodded, running his fingers along his combover as he offered a crooked-toothed smile. "What can I do for ya?"

"Actually, I'm hoping you can answer a few questions for me."

Anson stuffed his hands into the pockets of his dingy cargo shorts, rocking back on his heels. Everything about him—from his baggy shorts to his Hawaiian shirt and unkempt chest hair creeping out from the undone top button—screamed that this guy didn't have a care in the world. It made Dana's stomach knot. Could people really be so cold blooded? Ritualist murders one day, smiling at adult expos the next? She began to doubt herself. Maybe this was where Barnes preyed on the desperate and lonely as he targeted his next victims.

A voice in the back of her mind resisted. Her parents wouldn't have come to a place like this, would they?

Again, she found herself wondering what secrets they'd kept from her.

"Shoot," Anson said, his rotten grin in place.

Shepard got down to business, rattling off the dates of the Romeo and Juliet murders. "Can you tell me where you were on those dates?"

"That depends. Who wants to know?"

Jake pulled his badge. "Agent Shepard, FBI. Is there somewhere we can speak privately?"

The color drained from Anson's ruddy face right before he bolted.

"Stop!" Jake took off after him, but that only seemed to make the oily little man move faster.

Dana was on the move, too. Innocent people didn't run. There was no way she was letting Barnes get away.

She tore off her stilettos and joined Shepard as they raced after him. But Barnes seemed just as desperate to escape as Dana was for answers. Every time it seemed like they were gaining on him, he'd evade them, knocking over anyone who got in his way. Once he was out of the massive ballroom that housed the expo, he only gained more ground, moving through the hotel like he'd grown up there.

When Barnes led Jake into the casino, she took a different path. Moving along the outside, she kept her eyes on the man who owed her answers. Jake was hot on his heels, but panicked patrons kept getting in his way.

In no time, Barnes was through the casino, into the lobby and out the front doors. The screech of tires gave Dana momentary hope that he'd been hit. She didn't want him dead, just slowed down. When she saw the angled cars and faces of worried drivers, she knew she hadn't gotten that lucky.

Shepard raced under the portico a moment after Dana. Surveying the scene, he roared at the onlookers. "Which way did he go?"

A valet pointed. Dana's heart was pounding in her ears as Jake lifted his phone to his mouth, yelling into it. "Suspect spotted. In pursuit on foot. Westbound on Harmon Ave." A second later the phone was in his pocket and Shepard's hand was around Dana's. "Come on. Let's get this bastard."

21

Dana bent at the waist, her hands on her knees as she tried to catch her breath.

The ice cold air-conditioning inside the Cosmopolitan Hotel chilled her sweat, making her shiver. She wasn't out of shape. The damn skintight jumpsuit just wasn't built for running. But that hadn't stopped her from sprinting down the Strip in pursuit of Barnes.

She blamed her wheezing on the staggering Nevada heat. Her sweat-slicked palms slipped against the pleather as she tugged at the tight material. She could barely take a full breath with the way the jumpsuit was crushing her ribs.

Dana swore under her breath, wishing she could just rip the ridiculous costume off.

"You okay?" Shepard asked.

She glared at him. "Why didn't you shoot him?"

"You don't draw your weapon unless you intend to use it. And I couldn't very well take a shot in a crowded public place. Besides, we don't even know if he's guilty."

"He ran! That conveys guilt."

"Well lucky for him, you don't get to play judge, jury and executioner. It's innocent until proven guilty, Doc."

"I know that! It's just ..."

"Just what?"

"I need answers."

"Are you ready to tell me why this case is so important to you?"

Before she'd decided how to answer, Shepard's phone buzzed in his pocket. He picked it up, nodding as he grunted a response she couldn't hear. When he hung up, his stern gaze moved to Dana. "Stay here."

"Are you kidding me? I didn't track this guy across the country and run barefoot down Las Vegas Boulevard to stand by and let you get all the glory. I'm going in with you."

"Negative. We don't know if Barnes is armed. I can't let you go in there. It's too dangerous."

"What about you?"

"Don't worry about me." He gave her a patronizing smirk and patted his weapon. "Besides, I have back up."

Dana looked at the officers gathered in the Cosmopolitan Hotel. They all stood at the ready, awaiting Agent Shepard's orders. Barnes had been seen entering one of the clubs inside the flashy hotel. They lucked out in the fact it was a nightclub, so it was empty of patrons and employees at this hour. According to hotel security, there was only one way in and out. This could be their big break.

Dana stared at the neon glow of the giant red key next to the club entrance. She'd spent half her life researching symbolic artifacts. It made it hard not to think of the club's logo as a sign. Was this red key about to unlock the questions that had plagued her for a lifetime?

Her body thrummed with anticipation as she watched Shepard dole out tactical instructions. He moved about the officers with authority, taking only seconds to put together a swift and precise attack. It was clear he was in his element here. Dana was not. Recognizing that, she took a step back and let the professionals do what they did best. It was the same respect she hoped Shepard would show her if they'd found themselves in some satanic ritual site rather than a police standoff.

Heart in her throat, Dana silently wished Shepard and the officers luck as they made their move into the club, praying they'd all come out alive and with the answers she desperately needed.

The minutes dragged on like a Pennsylvania winter, harsh and unrelenting. If this kept up, Dana wasn't going to have any fingernails left. Normally, she shoved her hands in her pockets to curb the nervous habit, but her damn skintight jumpsuit didn't have any. She couldn't stand this, just waiting outside when the man behind the black double doors in front of her might've killed her parents.

Dana felt useless, and that was one thing she hated more than not knowing the truth.

She knew Shepard was right, it would be dangerous for her to enter unarmed, but in her experience the mind could be a deadly weapon, and hers was as sharp as any blade.

The red key glowed, neon pulsing as if inviting her in. The pop of gunfire made Dana's decision for her. Ignoring the protests of two officers who'd remained outside with her and hotel security, Dana made a run for it.

She rushed through the doors, stumbling into an alternate reality.

The darkness of the retro speakeasy club was disorienting. She pressed her back into a wall of vinyl records, giving her eyes a moment to adjust before moving through the strange room. Crouched, she moved past an old Victrola and crates of booze labeled 'confiscated'. She navigated the worn velvet seating and made her way down a hall lined with prohibition repeal posters to a heavy wooden door leading to the main club. It had a sliding iron peephole, which had been left half open. Just enough for her to get a glimpse inside.

All was quiet. Too quiet. Like the lull between waves on a deserted beach. She was sure she'd heard gunfire, but she saw no sign of movement inside the club. No one writhing on the floor in pain, no suspect in custody.

For a full minute she held her breath, listening for any signs of life. Her senses tingled, telling her this was a bad idea, but her heart wouldn't let her turn back. Silently pushing the door open, Dana made her way into the belly of the massive nightclub.

The space spanned at least two floors from what she could see, maybe more. The floor she was on split into varying levels and dark alcoves. It was the perfect place to hide. Shepard had only gone in with six officers, but a place this size would take three times that many men to canvass. It confirmed Dana's decision to disobey him. In a space like this, Shepard needed all the help he could get.

Staying low, she moved past a white baby grand piano into a room with a massive backlit stained-glass window. The light cast an eerie green and yellow glow across the empty tables and marble floor. Slipping into one of the curtained alcoves, Dana took a minute to survey the area.

Across the room was a long bar in front of a mirrored wall displaying a row of expensive liquor. The bottles glowed as the neon lights of the bar faded from blue to pink to yellow and back again. Plastic crates of clean glassware sat on the black granite bar top, waiting for the barback to come in and stow them away.

Everything seemed in its place.

Her eyes traveled along the bar one more time, a row of large glass terrariums snagging her attention. What a strange item to have in a nightclub. The grouping of empty domed glasses on the bar reflected the light from the barback mirror in an unnerving way. The shadows behind them almost seemed to take on a life of their own.

For some reason, she couldn't tear her eyes away. Dana's gaze fixed on a familiar sliver of bright material that rose and fell into view inside the glass as though it was breathing. That's when it hit her. The shadows behind the glass terrariums looked unnatural because they were. The concave glass was reflecting an odd angle of the mirror that normally wouldn't be visible.

Hope rose so swiftly in her chest it was hard to breathe. Suppressing her eagerness, Dana stood slowly, her eyes never leaving the unmistakable pattern of the Hawaiian shirt. She'd recognize it anywhere, even through the distorted looking glass. Keeping her movements slow, she crept toward Barnes' hiding place. Sheltering behind the bar had been a mistake. It may have kept him from sight, but Dana had the advantage now. His view of her approach would be blocked unless he gave up his cover.

A few more steps and she would be there. Her heart pounded so loudly in her ears she almost didn't hear her mistake, but Barnes did.

His head shot up from behind the bar the moment her foot made contact with the chair leg. It squeaked across the marble floor. Barnes bolted like a horse from a starting gate, and Dana had no option but to give chase.

"Stop!" she screamed, racing after him.

Barnes cleared the bar, and darted through the club, flipping chairs in his wake to slow her down, but Dana wasn't deterred. Her eyes locked onto the back of his head like a heat-seeking missile. Lungs burning, she pushed herself hard, following him down a level. Her conviction didn't seem to matter, Barnes was just plain faster. But Dana didn't give up and it paid off.

She got her first break when he turned down a hall and tripped on a riser he hadn't seen in the dark. The change in floor level sent him sprawling. It was all she needed to close the distance between them. She never broke stride as she flung herself onto his back. Her knee connected with his spine with so much force it knocked the wind out of him, giving Dana the advantage she needed to gain control. Twisting his arms behind his back, she pinned him to the ground.

Chest heaving, she hissed out the words she needed to say. "Did you do it? Did you kill them?"

"What the hell are you talking about, lady?"

"James and Renee Gray." She rattled off the date and location her parents' bodies had been found with the practice of one's own birthday and home address. Tears blurred her vision, but she didn't let that stop her. Wrenching his arms painfully, she demanded an answer. "Tell me the truth! You owe me that."

"I didn't kill nobody, lady! Christ! Get off me."

Dana began rattling off the names of the most recent victims, but that only infuriated Barnes further. "You're not pinning this on me. I'm no murderer!"

He began to buck and kick, but Dana held tight.

It wasn't good enough.

Barnes tore an arm free and elbowed her in the ribs. She lost her leverage and he rolled her off of him. In a flash she'd lost control, and now it was his turn for revenge.

He swung wildly, one of his fists connecting with her jaw.

Dana tasted blood, but she wasn't going down without a fight. She centered herself, letting her mind slip into her taekwondo training. Barnes came at her with another punch, but she blocked it with a kick and scrambled back to her feet. Barnes came at her again. This time she snapped a front kick into his shins. He groaned in pain, but didn't stop coming at her with his fists. And now he was ready for her.

Anticipating her next kick, Barnes dodged the knee strike that should've dropped him. He grabbed Dana by the hair, shoving her into the wall while she was off balance. She saw stars after her head met drywall, but Barnes wasn't done yet. His fist still tightly wrapped in her hair, he yanked her head back, disabling her with a chokehold. He was breathing heavily, his mouth next to her ear. "You've got the wrong guy, bitch. I'm not who you—"

Whatever he'd been about to say was interrupted by shouts from down the hall. Dana turned toward the sound of Shepard's voice.

"Over here!" she screamed. "Barnes is over here!"

Barnes let go of her and tried to bolt, but Dana clung to him. He struggled against her hold, dragging her a few steps down the hall before he turned back, apparently done messing around. He drew a gun from somewhere in his cargo shorts and grabbed her by the throat. She stared down the barrel, unblinking. The only thought in her head —*do it! Pull the trigger! End this torture for good.*

22

Red and blue lights flashed, making Dana's head hurt even worse. The last thing she remembered was the sound of Barnes' footsteps fleeing as the world went fuzzy around the edges before disappearing. Now she sat on the tailgate of an ambulance, her bare feet tapping on the warm Las Vegas pavement impatiently while Shepard conferred with Bishop and some other officials from the hotel.

Dana knew she was lucky to be alive, but she didn't feel that way. Barnes was gone and so was their only lead in this case, taking her last hope of solving her parents' murder. She closed her eyes and saw the barrel of the gun again. It frightened her that in the moments when her life should've flashed before her eyes, she saw nothing but emptiness. It wasn't all that surprising. That's what her life had been—empty. Her parents' killer had seen to that.

Ever since she lost them, she'd lived on nothing but the hope of avenging them. Now she didn't even have that to cling to. She'd finally come to the conclusion that if the FBI couldn't catch some scrawny porn peddler, her chances of unraveling a nearly twenty-year-old cold case was hopeless.

Dana found herself wishing Barnes had just pulled the trigger rather than pistol whipped her. It was a morbid thought, and it frightened her. But she was desperate to make the hurt stop.

For years she'd learned to bury it just deep enough that she'd fooled herself into thinking she was living a normal life. But when Agent Shepard walked into her life with his nearly identical crime, all those painful memories came rushing back to the surface. It reminded Dana that she'd been living a lie. There was nothing normal about her or the fact that she'd dedicated her life to solving her parents' murder. Worse than that was she might have to face the fact that maybe there was nothing to solve, and that her years of research into the occult had all been a waste of time.

That thought was even more depressing than the fact that she'd let Barnes slip through her hands. Dana tenderly pulled the ice pack from her head, feeling the egg sized welt just behind her right ear. From the corner of his eye, Shepard caught her wince and finished up his conversation.

He wore his concern like a badge as he strode over. "How are you feeling?"

"Ridiculous," she grumbled, looking down at the absurdly sexy black jumpsuit she still wore. It only added insult to injury.

The brief curve of Shepard's lips didn't make her feel any better. But the fact that he was still wearing a t-shirt with a pinup girl on it did. "You ready to get out of here?" he asked.

Dana arched her brows, then winced from the unexpected pain. "What do you mean? Are we leaving? Without Barnes?"

She tried to get to her feet, ready to protest, but her vision danced, and she reached out for the side of the truck. As usual, Shepard was there to steady her, but she batted him away. She knew better than to get used to having someone to lean on. She sat down, feeling defeated.

Sighing, Shepard joined her. "Listen, this isn't over, but the best thing we can do right now is let the Vegas PD do their job. I have a ton of paperwork to fill out thanks to your stunt." His intense blue eyes sharpened on her. "I don't suppose you want to tell me why you disobeyed a direct order?"

Dana started to shake her head, instantly regretting it. "I wasn't thinking."

"You got that right," he muttered.

Rising to his feet, Shepard extended a hand. "We can talk about it after you've had some rest."

Dana hesitated, testing his patience. Shepard ran a hand through his hair, making the short, dark pieces stand at awkward angles. It made him look more relaxed even though he was anything but. "Dana, we're gonna get this guy, I promise you that. Bishop and his team are on it. We can start fresh and join them again in the morning, okay?"

Dana knew Shepard was right. She was useless right now. Her head throbbed, and every muscle in her body ached thanks to the beating she'd taken from Barnes. She didn't even want to see what she looked like. If it was even half as bad as she felt, she probably resembled roadkill.

For once, she reluctantly took the help that was being offered. Dana reached up for Shepard's hand and followed him to an unmarked squad car ready to take them back to their hotel where she could lick her wounds.

23

Jake drew the phone to his ear reflexively, not even bothering to look at the time. He already knew it was an ungodly hour, which meant the call was important. "Shepard."

"Shep? It's Cramer."

Jake sat up, rubbing the sleep from his eyes. He cleared his throat. "What is it?"

"Barnes isn't your guy."

Heart sinking, Jake asked what he already knew the answer to. "Fresh scene?"

"Yeah. I just arrived. Same signature. Two bodies, vials, satanic shit."

Jake held in his sigh. "All right. When do we fly out?"

"Check with HQ, but it might be faster to catch something commercial depending on how quickly they can put a flight plan together."

"Understood."

"Call me when you land."

"Roger that."

Jake disconnected the call and flipped on the bedside lamp. The clock read 4:28 AM. At least he'd gotten a little shut-eye. Not much, but still better than nothing.

He'd been up until well after midnight filling out paperwork from the Barnes fiasco. Not wanting to bother with more, he put in a call to his secretary to book him and Gray on the next commercial flight out of Vegas, and then took a quick shower to wake himself up.

He wasn't looking forward to waking Dana up and telling her they were leaving Vegas and Barnes behind. After the stunt she pulled, he was more convinced than ever that she was hiding something. His uncle's words floated back to him. *People don't run into burning buildings unless there's something inside calling them.*

Jake hadn't yet figured out what it was about this case that was calling to Dana. Still, he had to admit, she continued to impress him. He was pissed that she'd disobeyed him and put herself in danger like that, but it took guts to go after Barnes the way she had. From the bruises he'd seen forming on her knuckles, he had a feeling that she'd given as good as she got.

As Jake dipped his head under the hot water, letting the slow burn bring him back to life, his thoughts trailed back to Dana in that Black Widow jumpsuit. It was too easy to picture her here in the shower with him. An ache built inside him as he imagined his hands slowly gliding over her curves, peeling the wet black material from her pale skin.

"Shit ..." Jake cranked the faucet to cold and forced himself to think of anything except the gorgeous librarian.

It'd been a while since he'd let anyone get under his skin—or under his sheets for that matter—but he was determined to keep things professional. It made him even more eager to get back to DC and wrap up this case. Then he'd be rid of Dr. Gray and this unwanted distraction.

By the time Jake was toweling off, his phone blinked with a new email showing their flight itinerary out of McCarran. He picked up the phone to let Gray know the change of plans. When she didn't answer, something akin to dread found a way into his gut.

Taking his gun from the safe, he tucked it in the waistband of his joggers as he rushed to the door. He'd been in too much of a hurry to check on her to bother pulling on a shirt. The cold temperature in the hall made his skin tighten with goosebumps.

Silently moving toward her room, Jake stopped outside Gray's door, rapping loudly. "Dana? Dana, are you in there?"

He was met with silence. Swearing, he knocked again, louder this time. She'd better be in there. He wouldn't put it past her not to let this thing with Barnes go. If she'd gone off and done something stupid ...

The sound of the lock tumbling stopped his train of thought. The door cracked open an inch and Dana peered out, the lock guard still in place. It calmed Jake's nerves that she had the sense to use it.

Her dark eyes widened as she blinked back at him. "Jake? What's wrong?"

"Change of plans. We're going back to DC."

"DC? When?"

"Now. Get dressed. Our plane leaves at 0600."

He turned to walk back to his room, but heard Dana's door shut just long enough for her to unbolt the guard.

"Shepard! Wait!" The door swung open and Dana followed him into the hall, skimpy pajamas and all. "What's going on?"

Jake turned back to face her, doing his best to keep his eyes on her face and not the thin cotton of her sleep shirt or how high up her thighs the hem hit. "We can't talk about it here. I'll tell you on the plane."

"What about Barnes?"

"He's not our guy."

"You don't know that!"

"Actually, I do." Understanding flashed across her pale face, making her bruises aggravate him even more. This woman had already been through enough. He never should've brought her into the field. Jake turned away, but Dana's words called him back.

"Maybe he's not our guy, but he's not innocent either or he wouldn't have run."

"Well, he's not our problem now."

Dana's mouth fell open. Her outrage was endearing. Jake remembered when he was like that—believing justice would always prevail. But that was a long time ago, before he joined the Army and found out how unjust the world truly was.

"He'll resurface, Dana. And when he does Bishop and his guys will bring him in."

Jake turned away from Dana's wounded expression and headed back to his room before that appealing outrage of hers wormed its way in so deep that he would feel like that old version of himself again. The one that craved more than the comfort of a warm body now and again.

24

Wincing, Dana did her best to cover the bruises on her face with the little makeup she'd brought with her. She'd never really cared much about her looks, but she sure didn't love the purple bruising under her eyes.

It was worth it, though. Each scrape and bruise was a badge of honor if she'd inflicted even an ounce of the pain she'd felt her whole life onto the monster who'd taken her parents from her.

But had she?

Something still bothered her about Anson. He was a class A criminal—she was sure of that—but she wasn't convinced he'd killed her parents. It was stupid, but she thought she'd feel something when she locked eyes with the person who stole so much from her. But with Anson ... she'd felt nothing.

Forcing away her nagging suspicions, she focused on covering up just how much going after Anson had cost her.

When she was satisfied, Dana stood back and studied herself in the mirror. Not bad. But not good either. It would have to do. She needed to meet Shepard in the lobby soon or they'd miss their flight back to DC.

Sighing, she sat on the edge of the bathtub to put on her shoes. Her feet were killing her after running barefoot for half a dozen blocks tracking Barnes.

And all for nothing.

Dana pushed away her self-pity and pain. Bruises would fade. Her grief would not. That's what had compelled her to go into the nightclub after Barnes.

Shepard had ripped her a new one over it.

He told her no one had discharged a weapon, so he wasn't buying that she'd heard a gunshot. Honestly, she couldn't be sure she'd heard one either. She'd been acting on pure adrenaline.

Going after Barnes by herself was stupid. She knew that. But she also knew she'd do it all over again if it meant she had another chance to bring him down.

Locking her anger away, Dana finished dressing. She found her mind wandering back to Shepard and the look of concern in his eyes when he'd knocked on her door earlier. It wasn't fair that he looked so gorgeous at such an ungodly hour. Dana felt like a zombie, but Jake looked like one of the Greek statues displayed at their hotel. She'd always known he was fit, but when he'd shown up wearing nothing but dog tags and jogging pants, she'd been momentarily speechless.

It wasn't just his perfect six pack that caught her attention, it was the scars that covered him like a patchwork of pain.

It made her wonder if she'd misjudged him. Dana wore her pain like a shield, but maybe Jake buried his. She wasn't sure either way was healthy, but it made them who they were, for better or worse.

25

Jake strained against his seatbelt, looking past Dana for one last glimpse out the window at the Nevada landscape. The sun was just rising, making the haze shrouding the Spring Mountain range shimmer in the distance. The palm trees lining the runway shrunk to the size of lollipops, dotting the packed brown earth until they gave way to the grid pattern of neighborhoods, then desert.

As the plane climbed higher, Jake's thoughts of a family reunion faded. It made him glad he hadn't reached out to his mother or Wade while he was in town. They would only be disappointed having known he was so close, yet still so far away.

Dana gave him a quizzical look when she caught him staring at the bland landscape a bit too long. He looked away, but not soon enough.

"Are you okay?" she asked.

"Fine."

"You don't look fine. You look ... forlorn."

Jake smirked. "How many points does that word get you?"

She cocked her head.

"You know, in crosswords."

"How should I know?"

He shrugged. "You look like someone who does crosswords."

"I do, but words don't score you points in crosswords. You're thinking of Scrabble."

Jake huffed a laugh, shaking his head at the ridiculousness of their conversation. They were chasing a serial killer and here they were talking about board games. He supposed it was partially his fault. Dr. Gray might be a genius in all things occult, but she was just as good at keeping people at arm's length as he was. If they were ever going to learn to work together, one of them was going to have to crack.

A glance at Gray and her bruised cheek told Jake everything he needed to know. She was too stubborn to make the first move. Hell, she'd gotten her ass handed to her yesterday, and she still hadn't admitted why she was so invested in this case. He was going to have to be the one to break the ice.

Sighing, he went for his preferred approach—ripping off the Band-Aid. "My family lives here."

Gray lowered her sunglasses, hitting him with the full power of those soulful brown eyes of hers. "Really? You're from Las Vegas?"

"Ellsworth. A few miles outside the city."

"Huh."

He laughed. "Huh? That's all I get?"

"Sorry, I'm still trying to process it."

"Process what?"

"The fact that you're from Vegas."

"Ellsworth," he corrected. "Why's that so hard to believe?"

"You don't look like a Nevadan."

It was his turn to arch his brows. "Oh, are you a profiler now?"

Her full lips curved up into what could almost be considered a smile, but it disappeared so fast Jake wasn't sure if he imagined it.

Man, she was a tough nut to crack. He was going to have to give her more. "I haven't seen them in a while; my family. My mother and my Uncle Wade still live in Ellsworth. It's a little spit of a town near a military base. I'd hoped I might have time to get up there and see them if things had worked out differently with Barnes."

"Are you close with them?"

Jake was mid nod before he realized that wasn't true. "I used to be."

"What happened?"

This was it, his moment to extend the olive branch. But that was easier said than done. Jake's hands shook as his mind brought him back to that moment. The moment that had finally broken him. "My last tour in Ghazni ... I lost someone ... a teammate."

But Ramirez was more than that. Jake's throat tightened as he thought about his best friend. "We grew up together." Gripping the armrests to stop his hands from shaking, Jake forced himself to continue. "I guess it's hard to go back home knowing he can't."

Jake slowly shook his head, the last images of his best friend flashing through his mind; the charred remains of their Humvee, the stench of burnt flesh ...

Dana's soft voice brought him back. "It doesn't feel like home without him there."

Her words surprised him. Jake turned to meet her solemn gaze. Those sad eyes of hers ... they looked like they'd lived a thousand lives worse than his. Yet somehow, she comforted him. Making him feel like he wasn't alone in his misery. Jake nodded. "Exactly. I don't think it'll ever be home again without him."

"What was his name?"

Jake swallowed, his vocal cords feeling as though they'd snap as he forced the name out. "Ramirez. Danny Ramirez." Out of habit Jake put his hand to his chest, making sure the dog tags he always wore were still there. There were three on the stainless-steel ball chain around his neck. A man he looked up to, a man he never wanted to turn into, and a man he'd never forget.

"You wear his dog tag," Dana said, matter-of-factly. At Jake's bewildered expression, she offered a hint of a smile. "I saw it this morning when you came to my room. You weren't wearing a shirt."

"Oh. Right." Jake was going to say more, but the faint blush that crept into Dana's cheeks distracted him.

"Who are the others for?"

Jake let his hand drop from his chest, returning it to the arm rest. "Maybe I'll tell you some other time."

Feeling Dana's hand slide over his surprised him. "I'd like that," she said, her hand giving a slight squeeze before returning to her lap.

Jake returned her smile. This time he knew he hadn't imagined it. It had been a genuine one, and it put him at ease. Reclining his seat, he closed his eyes and let sleep pull him under. With the way this case was going, he had a feeling he'd need it.

Talking about Ramirez had drained him. He hadn't spoken his best friend's name out loud since his debriefing years ago. As he drifted to sleep, Jake wondered if he was mistaking exhaustion for progress.

26

Dana watched Shepard sleep on the flight home, wondering what he was dreaming about behind his flickering eyelids. She hoped it wasn't Ramirez. She felt bad that she'd inadvertently picked at an old wound.

Listening to Shepard talk about his friend was the first chink she'd seen in his armor. Though he hadn't gone into detail about what happened, Dana knew enough about what went on in the combat zones of Afghanistan to know it had most likely been horrific. Especially if it scarred a man like Jake Shepard.

The more time she spent with him, the less she believed the story he told her that first day at the crime scene. She appreciated that he'd felt the need to do her a kindness in her moment of weakness, but she needed him to know she wasn't in the habit of being weak or needing rescue. Dana had grown up fast, feeding herself a steady diet of vengeance, ensuring her heart was hewn of steel so that when she got the chance to avenge her parents, she wouldn't hesitate.

That's why she was so upset with herself over Anson Barnes. She'd had him right there. And if it hadn't turned out that he wasn't the killer, she never could've lived with herself knowing she let him slip through her grasp.

Shepard filled her in on his conversation with Cramer on the drive to the airport. The new crime scene in DC was enough to exonerate Barnes, but it still irked her that she wouldn't be there when the creep was brought to justice. He may not be the Romeo and Juliet killer, but Dana was convinced he wasn't an innocent man.

She winced as her hand brushed the tender bruise on her cheek. Dana wanted to press charges, but Shepard advised against it. Based on her statement, he said it sounded like she got in just as many shots on Barnes and with no other witnesses, it'd be his word against hers. Shepard told her pressing charges would be like poking a hornet's nest and not worth the headache.

Dana hated the idea of letting Barnes off, but Shepard promised her he'd go down for his pirating charges, along with a few others that Vegas PD were waiting to pin on him for the mayhem he'd caused in the nightclub. She wanted to believe Shepard, but it wasn't easy. Dana glanced over at the sleeping FBI Agent again, wondering just how much she could trust the man. So far, he'd been upfront with her about everything.

Okay, maybe not the rookie crime scene story, but the ends justified the means.

It'd be a whole lot easier to work with Shepard if she didn't have to hide the truth from him. Based on the striking similarities of the cases, telling him about what happened to her parents might even help. But she was torn. They'd only known each other a few days. A crazy few days, but still ... Dana had kept this secret for almost twenty years. Keeping something trapped inside that long made it intimate and hard to let go.

Her gaze moved from his cleanly shaven face to his blue dress shirt, her mind drifting back to the perfect specimen of sculpted muscles that lay beneath. Her cheeks warmed. She couldn't deny that he was attractive. She'd have to be dead not to feel something sitting this close to the man, but that only made telling him the truth more difficult. Sharing her story with Jake would feel like giving him a part of her. And that was something she just didn't do.

27

BLUE AND RED LIGHTS STROBED HARSHLY IN DANA'S VISION, WARNING HER she didn't want to see what was inside the cheap motel. She followed Shepard toward the crime scene anyway.

She wasn't sure she'd ever get used to walking toward police lights. It seemed ingrained in human nature to heed the warning of police tape and keep away.

Dana had seen more police in the past forty-eight hours than she ever wanted to. And once again, she found herself ducking under more yellow crime scene tape, wondering why she hadn't gone into law enforcement. Maybe a gun and badge would've been more useful than her collection of PhDs when it came to avenging her parents.

The smell of death hung heavy in the air as they approached the scene. Dana was prepared this time. Not only did she know what she'd most likely find in the hotel room, but she had an oversized sweatshirt to duck her head into if things got too overwhelming. She picked it up at the airport while waiting to board the plane. It was navy blue and proclaimed, 'What happens in Vegas, Stays in Vegas,' in large yellow letters. Jake told her she looked absurd, but she didn't care. The airport was freezing, and the flight had been even colder. And now, back in DC, she was grateful for the cozy layer of protection against the macabre chill in the air.

Cramer met them at the door to room 213. It was open wide, the click and flash of the crime scene photographers cutting through the stillness. It puzzled Dana that they were still at the crime scene. According to Jake, Cramer called him at four in the morning. *Shouldn't most of the forensics team be finished by now?*

Jake seemed to be wondering the same thing. "Why's forensics still here?"

Cramer waved him off. "Got in a pissing match with the DEA. Don't get me started. The important thing is the scene is ours. Come on, I'll walk you through it."

Cramer waited while Jake and Dana donned blue paper booties and latex gloves. His steel gray eyes appraised her the entire time. The hairs on the back of Dana's neck rose. She didn't like the way the commanding agent's gaze lingered on her. Shaking it off, she put on her game face and followed Jake into the hotel room.

The scene was just as she expected. Twin beds. Two victims. Woman on the left, man on the right, each with an empty poison vial in their hands folded neatly over their chests. Between both beds on the bland oatmeal carpet was a large blood-soaked pentagram. This one had four of the five points filled in.

As Dana stared at it, the world began to sway. She quickly backed out of the room while Cramer and Shepard continued examining the evidence. Out in the hallway, Dana gulped down cool air. She wrapped her arms tightly around herself as she waited for her breathing to return to normal. She would never get used to this. But maybe that was a good thing. Maybe it meant she wasn't as hardened as she'd hoped to be.

A lifetime of studying rituals of death, and she still wasn't prepared to face the real thing. Dana shook her head, steeping in self disappointment. Still, this time had gone better than the last. At least she'd made it out of the hotel room on her own two feet.

She'd seen all she needed to. There were two more victims. That told her everything she needed to know. The killer was still out there, and she'd failed—again.

28

"HOW'S DR. GRAY HANDLING THIS?"

Jake shoved his hands in his pockets, feeling more like himself after a few nights in his own bed. He leaned against Cramer's office wall while the man sat at his desk sipping coffee. Jake shrugged. "As well as can be expected."

Cramer frowned. "I wouldn't call what happened in Vegas 'expected'."

Jake did his best to hide the pride that bubbled up inside him. "Yeah. She surprised us all taking on Barnes like that."

"You heard Vegas PD apprehended him?"

"I did."

"Are we certain he wasn't involved in any of this?" Cramer asked.

"As certain as we can be right now. But if that changes, we know where he'll be. He's being held without bond until his hearing."

"Good. Let's try to avoid surprises from now on. I need you to keep that woman in one piece. She's on loan to us from the Smithsonian. I can only imagine the shitstorm we'd be in if something happened to her while in our care."

"Don't worry, Cap. I'm keeping an eye on Dana."

"Dana?" Cramer's frown deepened. "You two are on a first name basis?"

Jake shrugged. "Is that a problem?"

"No. As long as you're not crossing any lines."

"Whoa!" Jake held his hands up, insulted by the insinuation. "I know better than to fish off the company dock."

Cramer chuckled. "Glad to hear it."

"Damn, Cramer. I thought you knew me."

"I do. But I know the lure of an attractive woman as well. I saw the way you were looking at her when she left the scene."

"She got a little dizzy the last time. I just wanted to make sure it didn't happen again. Especially considering the knock to the head she took in Vegas."

"How is she recovering?"

"I'm sure the few days off did her good. I'm heading over to meet with her now. I want to fill her in on Barnes and hear about this new theory she has for me on the case."

"She has a new lead?"

"Maybe. Something about Mercutio or something Shakespearean?"

Cramer's eyebrows rose.

"I know. Half the time I'm not even sure what language she's speaking, but I've never seen someone so determined to crack a case. Wish we had a few more agents like her."

"Be careful," Cramer warned, his tone icy. "There is no darkness but ignorance."

Jake gave the old Army captain an odd look.

He grinned. "She's not the only one who can quote Shakespeare."

Jake shook his head as he left Cramer's office. This case was full of strange surprises. First, he found himself with a vigilante librarian for a partner, and now his boss was reciting poetry. Jake liked to think outside the box, but this was a little much, even for him.

124

29

Dana's phone buzzed in her pocket. When she saw it was Shepard, she nodded to Claire. "Put it on speakerphone so I don't lose my place."

Claire shuffled around the desk, one hand still holding the UV screened LED light over the manuscript Dana was deciphering. "Dr. Dana Gray's office," Claire sang into the phone.

Shepard's voice boomed through the office. "Is she there?"

Claire's eyes widened, as they always did at the first sign of trouble. Dana spoke up. "Yes, Shepard, I'm here. I'm glad you called. I was thinking—"

He interrupted her. "You're at work?"

"Of course."

"I'm at your house."

"Why?"

He exhaled loudly. "I thought the purpose of taking a few days off was for you to get some rest?"

"No rest for the wicked," she quipped.

"Dana, you have a head injury."

"Had," she corrected. "Besides, thinking is the best way to heal the mind."

"It takes more than a few days to recover from a knock like that. I would know."

Dana thought about the dog tags on the chain around Jake's neck and his friend who hadn't made it home. Even though Shepard had survived that last tour, she wondered what the price had been. Someday, she hoped he'd share the rest of the story with her.

She could admit she was curious about the other names he carried close to his heart. But for now, she'd have to wait to uncover the secrets he hid behind his desolate blue eyes. She had a murder investigation to solve.

And she was almost there. She could feel it.

"Never mind my head. I think I have another lead. How fast can you get here?"

After a lot of grumbling, Shepard agreed to come to the library. Claire disconnected the call and returned to her spot, but Dana didn't miss the way her intern's clear blue eyes sparked with questions.

"Is there something on your mind, Claire?"

"He calls you Dana now?"

"Yes. Is there a problem with that?"

She grinned. "What happened in Vegas?"

Dana sighed. "I told you what happened. Anson Barnes fled and—"

"Not with the case. With you and sexy Secret Agent Man."

"Claire. That's unprofessional."

"Oh come on. You can't tell me you don't think he's gorgeous."

Dana's thoughts conjured up images she was trying to suppress. Jake shirtless at her door, concern in his unwavering gaze. "We're just partners, Claire."

"Partners." Claire smirked as she rattled off the definition from memory. "Either of a pair of people engaged together in the same activity."

"That activity is catching a serial killer. Nothing more."

Claire's grin only grew. "If you say so."

AN HOUR LATER, Dana had Shepard engrossed in her newest theory. They sat huddled over their usual table on the library floor. This time, she had a different set of books spread out before them. Ones that she'd borrowed from the Smithsonian's Elizabethan department.

"They have to mean something," Dana argued, gesturing to the list she'd compiled.

Shepard disagreed. "I think you're reaching."

"The door numbers mean something. I'm sure of it."

"A few minutes ago, you were sure they represented lines in Shakespeare's sonnets, but we've been through these books so many times I'm going to end up reciting this nonsense in my sleep."

"You really think I'm wrong?"

"I think sometimes a door number is just a door number."

Dana's resolve crumbled. She'd been so sure she was on to something, but maybe Shepard was right. If she thought about it, the only reason she'd gone down the Shakespearean path was because of the name the media had created, sensationalizing their suspect as the Romeo and Juliet killer. She'd even taken it as far as calling the unsub Mercutio in her mind.

Sensing her frustration, Jake gave her shoulder a squeeze. "Why don't we take a break. Grab something to eat?"

Claire poked her head out of the stacks like a gopher coming out of a hole. "Did someone say food?"

Shepard stood up, stretching. "I was just telling Doc here we should take a break for lunch. You wanna join us?"

Claire's pale cheeks filled with color, leaving Dana to save her from her embarrassment. "Claire's not a fan of eating in public. Let's just order some takeout."

Shepard grumbled something under his breath but conceded. "Fine. We'll call something in." His concerned gaze settled on Dana again. "Wanna go for a ride with me to pick it up?"

She sat back, crossing her arms. "I don't need a break, Shepard. I'm fine."

He crossed his own arms, mimicking her as he met her glare. Claire's giggle broke their staring contest.

"Something funny?" Shepard snapped.

Claire surprised Dana by piping up. "For a soldier you're not very good at picking your battles."

The comment caught Dana so off guard she laughed. Even Shepard had a hard time keeping a straight face. Shaking his head, he threw his hands up. "All right, I know when I'm beat. I'm going to Thaiphoon. Call in whatever you want."

"What do you want?" Dana asked.

"I'll have whatever the smart ass is having. I at least like her taste in food."

After Shepard left, Claire sidled over and took up his seat, a wide grin lighting her normally serious face.

"What are you so happy about?"

Claire shrugged. "I didn't expect to like him."

"Who? Shepard?"

"Yeah. It's kinda nice having him around."

Dana's lips tugged up in the corners as she realized she almost agreed with Claire. She knew better than to say so. It wasn't a good idea to get attached. This arrangement was only temporary. She was about to remind her intern of that when Claire interrupted her by pointing to the sonnets and illustrations littering the table. "Did you find anything?"

Dana sighed. "I thought so, but Shepard shot holes in my Shakespeare theory."

Claire's eyes roamed the books with fierce curiosity. "What made you think it was related?"

Pushing her glasses up into her hair, Dana rubbed her eyes. "Honestly, I don't know. I'm just grasping at straws."

Maybe she did need a break. She was driving herself crazy trying to crack this code when there might not even be one. But she couldn't help thinking the FBI had come to her for a reason. She wanted to prove she could find the answers. But so far it felt like all she was doing was letting them down. And letting her parents down.

Claire's head cocked to an odd angle as her gaze froze on one of the crime scene photos that must've been dislodged from its folder while

Dana was shuffling sonnets around. Dana reached across the table to tuck it back in, but Claire stopped her. "Are all the scenes like this?"

"I'm sorry. I didn't mean to leave this out, Claire." Though it wasn't the first corpse the Egyptology student had seen, it was still disturbing.

"No, it's not that. It's just ..."

"What?"

"The woman on the right-hand side of the man. That's biblical, isn't it?"

A chill rippled through Dana. "Claire!" She grabbed her assistant's boney hands. "You are a genius."

Claire snatched her hands away, surprise etching her features as she clutched her wrists like Dana's touch had burned her.

"You okay?"

"Fine."

Dana knew the girl had quirks, but she'd never realized she was so uncomfortable with being touched. She studied her intern, briefly wondered if the girl had haphephobia, but Claire recovered quickly from whatever had startled her.

"I know I'm a genius." Her pale blue eyes blinked behind her thick glasses. "But why am I a genius in this scenario?"

"I don't know how I missed it. But you're right. If our killer was mimicking something Shakespearean, he would've had the woman on the left-hand side of the man, leaving his sword hand free to protect her. Almost all cultures practiced this custom, except in Christianity where Eve is depicted on Adam's right because she was carved from his right rib."

Adrenaline coursed through Dana's veins as she recalled something. She stood, staving off the wave of dizziness and spotty vision that accompanied the rapid movement. She didn't have time to baby her head injury. Forcing herself to focus, she made her way to the stacks. Her heart raced when she found the book she was looking for. Her fingers wrapped around the blue linen cover, and she knew she'd found the answer without even cracking the spine.

Dashing back to the table, Dana searched through the clutter and papers for her cell phone as Claire watched curiously. Finding it, she dialed Shepard's number, setting the phone down while it rang. Dana stroked the cover with shaking fingers before gaining the courage to open it. Though the book could be considered new compared to the other ancient tomes her floor of the library housed, Aleister Simon's controversial title had earned a place on the Smithsonian's occult floor.

When Shepard's phone went to voicemail, Dana hung up and tried again—four more times before she gave up and opened the book. She skimmed over the index and flipped through the back. Not finding what she was looking for, she grabbed her phone again and opened a browser, typing in various combinations of the title. Finally, she found it. She was shaking so badly she almost dropped her phone when it rang. Dana's pulse raced along with the melodic tone. "Shepard?"

"Did you really call me five times? If you were that hungry—"

"Jake! I figured it out! It wasn't Shakespearean at all. We should've been reading the Pentanic Verses of Satanism."

"Well yeah. I could've told you that, Doc. The pentagram kinda gave it away."

"No, that's the title. *The Pentanic Verses of Satanism.* It's a book. It was banned in several countries in the late eighties and nineties after provoking Muslim criticism. But as with all radical rantings, there are always as many for as against. The author, Aleister Simon, was forced into hiding after numerous assassination attempts. His supporters considered him a religious leader and went on to protest the ban, and subsequent burning of his books. When they were unsuccessful in overturning the ruling, they took his work of fiction into their own hands and formed the Pentacle Church in his honor, worshiping the three pagan goddesses he wrote about. They were three sisters, loosely based on the three fates of Greek mythology."

"I don't need a history lesson. Get to the point."

"I am. Simon's followers believed the three goddesses dedicated their lives to protecting their church and watching over its patrons, so they had no time to take lovers. Instead, lovers were brought to them."

"And let me guess, sacrificed?"

"Yes! The Pentacle Church practiced ritualistic human sacrifice. Always a male and female, symbolizing the lovers in Simon's writings.

It was thought an honor to volunteer for the sacrifice. Death by poison."

"And do we know their poison of choice?"

"Nightshade! It was chosen due to the star-shaped nature of the flower."

"Well done, Doc. This church ... are there any still operating?"

"Way ahead of you. There's only six Pentacle Churches still in existence worldwide because of their extreme beliefs. Guess where the closest one is?"

"I don't like guessing games."

"Maryland!"

Shepard grinned. "Then it looks like we're going on a little road trip."

30

Jake told Dana to pack a bag. Lunch would have to wait. He pulled out of Dupont Circle and headed back toward HQ to make the necessary arrangements and fill Cramer in on their plan.

"I thought you'd be pleased," Jake said, standing in his boss's office for the second time in one day. "You were right to bring her in on this case. Dana's lead is going to pay off this time. I can feel it."

Cramer stood from his desk, grabbed a pack of cigarettes out of his drawer, his steps heavy as he walked toward Jake. One hand on his shoulder, Cramer steered Jake toward the door.

"What's up, Cap?"

Cramer frowned. "We need to talk about Dr. Gray."

"I don't understand." Jake couldn't believe what he was hearing. "You think she's involved somehow?"

Cramer took a final drag from his cigarette before flicking it into the bushes. He exhaled the smoke slowly, savoring each poisonous vapor. Jake was glad he'd never taken up the disgusting habit, and he was surprised to see his boss had gone back to it after watching his brother beat cancer. Things must be dire.

"Look, Shep, I know you're attached to her, but the truth is, she can't be trusted."

"I'm not attached, and why are you just coming to me with this now?"

"It was need to know."

"Bullshit. My ass is on the line here, Cramer. I think that takes priority."

"I wanted to be sure first." Cramer pulled out his phone, and Jake felt his own vibrate. "I just sent you the file. The evidence is all right there. Dana Gray's parents died the same way as our current victims."

Jake took out his phone and opened the file Cramer sent, skimming the contents. It was all there, just like Cramer said. His eyes landed on the haunting crime scene photos—undeniable proof. Dana's parents were laid out in exactly the same way as the Romeo & Juliet victims. Jake recognized them from the photo she kept on her desk.

He fought against the betrayal that flared up inside him. "Why would she keep this from us?"

Cramer gave him a patronizing look. "What's the obvious reason?"

It couldn't be true. Dana wasn't a killer. But what reason would Cramer have to cast doubt in Jake's mind? "How did you find out about this?" When Cramer didn't answer, Jake swore. "You knew from the beginning, didn't you?"

He nodded. "It's why she was assigned to the case. We hoped she would lead us to anyone else involved."

Jake's blood boiled as he thought about the wild goose chase she'd led him on. "And no one thought this was something I needed to know?"

"It wasn't my call. But I'm telling you now."

Jake frowned. He was pissed. At Cramer. At the jackoffs in charge who kept him in the dark. But mostly at Dana. Still, he couldn't quite believe she was involved. He looked back through the file for anything to exonerate Dana, but Cramer was right. The evidence was damning.

"Come on," Cramer prodded. "You can't tell me you didn't wonder how she seemed to be one step ahead of us the whole time."

"What do you mean?"

"She figured out the poison without a toxicology report. She found the perfect patsy in Vegas and kept you busy while another murder took place."

"Well obviously she isn't the murderer, if that's your logic. Dana was with me the entire time in Vegas."

Cramer shrugged. "I didn't say I thought she was working alone."

Closing the encrypted file, Jake slipped his phone back into his pocket. "How do you want to play this?"

"Keep her on the case for now."

"You can't be serious?"

"A bird in hand ..."

"If Dana's involved, which I'm not entirely convinced of, she has every reason to obstruct our investigation."

"Not if she doesn't know we're on to her. Be patient. She'll slip up eventually, and I want you there to catch her when she does."

"So I'm supposed to just sit on the fact that I know her parents were murdered exactly the same way as our current vics?" Jake shook his head. "I don't like it."

"Luckily, you're not paid for your opinion."

Jake fought his urge to volley a sarcastic comeback. "We should look into this cold case. Finding out what happened to Dana's parents might shed some light on our current case."

"Her parents' deaths were ruled a murder-suicide; open and shut."

"Are we sure? Forensics have come a long way in the last twenty years. It might not be that simple."

"It never is. But that's not the play. You will sit on this information and continue your investigation as planned. That's an order."

Jake's jaw ached with agitation. He clamped it shut so hard he wouldn't be surprised if his teeth fell out in pieces when he spoke. But he didn't trust himself not to bite Cramer's head off for signing him up for this circus. Instead, he gave a sarcastic salute.

"Escort Dr. Gray to Maryland to look into the church. And take your time. We need you to keep her there while we get a warrant to search her apartment."

"Then what?"

"I'll let you know if there's reason to make an arrest."

"Anything else?"

"Just watch your back, Shep."

He laughed heartlessly. "I think I can handle a librarian."

Cramer gave him an appraising look. "Unless Maryland is just a ploy to get you to her next killing ground."

31

By the time they crossed state lines, Jake's feelings of betrayal had boiled into disgust. Mostly at himself for trusting this woman. He'd opened up to her, shared parts of his own tortured past, all while she sat next to him burying her own. He should've known better.

He honored loyalty and honesty above all else, and if Cramer was right about Gray, then she'd violated more than his trust. As far as Jake was concerned, anyone who was a party to these killings was the worst of humanity. And he had no mercy for the wicked.

"Are you sure you're okay?" Gray asked for what felt like the hundredth time.

Jake only nodded, not trusting his restraint. His temper had a short fuse. The last thing he needed to do was to lose control and call her out while in a moving vehicle. Especially in this downpour. He didn't need a rabbit on his hands.

Popping another piece of gum into his mouth, Jake gave his jaw something else to work, other than his rage.

Her gaze lingered on him a bit longer than necessary before she turned her attention back to the GPS. She was quiet. The only sound between them the squeak of the windshield wipers. It wasn't until Jake took an unprompted turn that she spoke again. "You weren't supposed to turn here. The GPS said to stay on 50 for a few more miles until the exit to our hotel."

"Yeah, I forgot to mention we need to make a stop first."

"Tonight?" Dana's dark eyes moved back to the clock on the dash. "It's late."

"It'll only take a minute."

JAKE PULLED the SUV into the parking lot of a rundown motel off 50 East and parked. It was a dive and the gloomy weather didn't do it any favors. This stop was off book and Cramer wouldn't like it. But Cramer wasn't here. It was Jake who had to share a hotel with a potential murder suspect. He needed to know if Gray was part of this or not.

Somewhere between leaving Cramer's office and picking her up, Jake had begun to suspect his boss might be right about her involvement. This seemed the fastest way to test that theory.

Grabbing his phone, Jake referenced a photo he'd saved to it. He held it up. Green roof, white siding, black wrought iron railings. *Yep, this was the place all right.*

The motel had changed names a handful of times in the past few years, but it still looked the same. Dingy and desolate.

Without a word, he got out of the car, knowing Gray would follow. She did. Jake kept his guard up as he walked toward the hotel. He'd decided it was best to think of Gray as guilty until proven innocent. And that part would be up to her.

What she revealed once inside the room he was taking her to would condemn or exonerate her. Either way, her fate was in her hands—even if she didn't know it yet.

32

Dana shook the rain from her coat and hair in the lobby. After Shepard flashed his badge to the man at the front desk, he was given a key to room 208. Dana followed him silently until they were alone in the stairwell. "What are we doing here?"

He didn't answer.

"Was there another murder?"

Still no answer.

A strange sense of déjà vu tickled her mind, making her wonder if Shepard was right about the severity of her head injury. Dana had only slept in fits and starts since returning from Las Vegas. She was exhausted and presently frustrated; a combination that trumped logic. She reached up and grabbed Shepard's arm, ready to demand an answer.

Not a smart move.

He moved so fast she was against the wall before she knew what happened. Her mind emptied of everything but fear as she clawed at his forearm. It was pressed against her windpipe, her other arm pinned painfully behind her back.

"Jake!" The word came out in a rasp. "What's going on?"

His face hardened as he brought his lips close to her ear, the smell of rain on his hot skin permeating the surrounding air. "You tell me."

Tears welled in her eyes. "I don't understand."

Somehow, her lack of answer satisfied him. Jake released her, stepping back to give her breathing room. Dana didn't know what the hell just happened, but she was grateful to breathe freely again.

She sucked in a breath, reflexively massaging her arm where his vice-like grip had been. If her confrontation with Barnes had rocked her confidence, this altercation with Shepard had decimated it.

Dana liked to think of herself as an independent woman who could defend herself if necessary. Staring at Shepard now, she was full of doubt. Had she been foolish to come here with him alone?

"Claire and everyone at the Smithsonian knows where I am tonight."

Shepard laughed. "Like you're the one who should be worried?"

"I don't understand. Please, just tell me what the hell is going on."

"Actually, I think you're the one who needs to start talking." He tried to push her up the stairs, but she wouldn't budge. "I'm not going anywhere with you until you explain yourself."

He let her go, shrugging. "I'll be in room 208. The explanation should be pretty clear."

Dana watched him go, his rugged silhouette swallowed up by the darkness. It was late and she was in the middle of nowhere with a hair-triggered FBI agent on a witch hunt. Maybe the case was getting to Shepard. The smart thing to do was to go back to the front desk and call her office. Or better yet, Agent Cramer. The FBI wouldn't leave her stranded out here if Shepard had actually snapped.

Standing in the stairwell, Dana looked back toward the first floor. Her good sense was pulling her in that direction, but she couldn't shake the nagging déjà vu that refused to let her leave this place. Reluctantly, she gave in to her curiosity and climbed the stairs.

She approached room 208 with caution. The door was open, foreboding filling the hallway. Dana's stomach knotted as she got closer. She saw the twin beds first. Her mind did the rest; memories filling in the blanks with bodies that weren't there. But that same patterned carpet was. She'd never forget it—dingy red with little gold starbursts.

Her feet moved her forward even though her mind was frozen in place, or maybe it was frozen in the past, because as she walked into the last room her parents had ever seen, all of Dana's nightmares came to life. Her heart was beating so fast she couldn't hear what Shepard was saying. She didn't care. She was finally here; in the place she'd lay awake imagining a million sleepless nights. The room where her parents left her.

Dana's knees slammed into the floor. She was vaguely aware of the pain, but her soul hurt so much worse. "Why?" she whispered. "Why did you leave me?"

What started out as a quiet plea turned into a sob as Dana hugged herself, rocking back and forth as tears streamed down her face. "Mom! Dad! Oh God. Why did you come here?"

Shepard must've thought her questions were meant for him, or maybe her hysterics were making him uncomfortable because he spoke, and she heard him this time. "I had to know for sure."

She looked up at him through her tears. "Know what?"

"If you were involved in this?"

"In what? My parents' murder?" Her voice was incredulous.

"Why didn't you tell me what happened to them?"

"I was afraid you'd throw me off the case if you knew I had a personal interest."

Jake swore under his breath. He ran his hands through his hair, spraying droplets of cold rainwater onto her. "I still might have to kick you off the case."

"Please don't!" Dana climbed to her feet, her heart pounding like a kick drum. It couldn't end here. Not like this. "We're close, Shepard. I need to see this through."

Looking morose, he shook his head, making no promises. "Let's go to our hotel. We can talk about it there."

"Wait!" Not having learned her lesson, she foolishly reached out to grab his arm again, but this time, he only stiffened. Between him and Claire, she was starting to get a complex. Shepard turned back to face her, his stormy gaze pinning Dana in place. She was testing his limits, she knew that, but being here had opened a new door for Dana. One that had always been locked until now. "This was the last place they were alive. I ... I need a minute to ... to say goodbye."

He nodded. "Take all the time you need." Then he walked out the door, giving her some privacy.

Dana took more than a few steadying breaths as she looked around the room. When she found her voice, she felt stupid, but she pushed past her embarrassment. Better to be a fool today than regret tomorrow. There was a yellow chair in the corner of the room. She walked toward it, thinking she'd sit down, but her mind filled the piece of furniture with the faceless shape of the killer.

Unable to bring herself to sit where her parents' murderer may have sat, Dana walked back to the center of the room, standing between both beds, near the foot. The bedspreads had been updated to crisp white linens, but otherwise, the room was exactly the same, right down to the art and the ugly red and gold carpet.

She swallowed past the tightness in her throat. It was raw from crying. She pushed past it. "Mom. Dad. I'm okay. I want you to know that. I love you. I've never stopped loving you. I don't believe for one second you left me by choice. I don't know why you were here. I don't care. But I'm not going to stop until whoever did this to you pays."

Fresh tears streaked over the dried tracks on her cheeks as she backed a few steps toward the door. "I love you," she whispered again. "And I'm going to make this right." Dana gave the room one last look.

Before leaving, her gaze landed on the worn yellow chair. She walked toward it, letting her fingers trail over the cigarette scarred dresser until she was close enough to touch the worn yellow fabric. "I'm coming for you," she warned the imaginary killer. "And I'm getting close."

With that, she left room 208 and closed the door on her haunted past. She hadn't known she would ever have the courage to face it, but now that she had, her determination to clear her family name was renewed. She was closing in on this monster; Dana could feel it. It was only a matter of time before she found him, but she had to wonder at what cost.

Though she'd survived, being thrown into her parents' crime scene unexpectedly had torn open old wounds, leaving her feeling shaken and fragile. The way Shepard had forced her to face her fears reminded her of the occult practice of trial by fire. The belief was weakness would be burned away, leaving only steel or ash. Dana wondered which she was. Steel or ash?

The only way to find out was to move forward, but she worried she wouldn't make it through in one piece if she tried to keep going it alone. It was time to share her burden and let someone in before there was nothing left of her.

Dana's gaze landed on Shepard. A few doors down, he leaned on the black wrought iron rail, looking out at the rain beating down on the pavement below. He looked as tattered as she felt. Squaring her shoulders, she walked toward him, knowing even together, there were no guarantees.

33

Jake stood outside watching the rain, feeling stupid for listening to Cramer.

He was glad he'd disobeyed orders and brought Dana here. He hated what he'd just put her through, but at least now he knew the truth. And that he could still trust his instincts.

Cramer was wrong.

There was no way Dana was involved in the killings. Jake would bet his life on it. He'd spent too many hours in interrogation rooms with terrorists he wasn't allowed to name to have the wool pulled over his eyes by a librarian. There was no doubt in his mind that Dana was innocent. What he'd just witnessed in that hotel room was proof. Her reaction to being thrown into her parents' old crime scene had been genuine.

All the signs were there. Jake had watched Dana's pulse points, tracked the way her pupils had dilated, measured her labored breaths. She exhibited all the signs of a person in shock. A person grieving, which was exactly what he'd left her to do. He owed her that.

Thoughts of Ramirez drifted into his mind. He always thought of him when it was raining like this. Like it had that day ... Except in Ghazni it had been blood that fell from the sky.

"Jake?" The sound of Dana's voice startled him back to the present.

He let go of the railing and stood upright. "Got everything you needed?"

"Not yet, but that'll have to do for now."

He gave her a nod, understanding what she meant more than she knew. "I'm sorry," he offered. "I wish there'd been another way, but I had to know if we were on the same team."

Her eyes narrowed. "The same team?" Understanding washed over her, instantly replaced by anger. "You think I had something to do with these murders?"

"Not here," Jake warned. "Come on."

"No." Dana stood her ground. "After what you just put me through, you owe me some answers. Now explain."

Jake released his frustration with a deep sigh. "This wasn't my idea."

"Then whose was it?"

"Cramer's."

"Why?"

"You have to admit it's suspicious. You've been one step ahead of us the whole time with the evidence and leads, and then when we found out your parents were killed in the exact same way ..."

"I'm confused. I thought you hired me for my expertise. Am I not supposed to tell you when I know the most likely poison or when I've identified a possible suspect?"

"Of course you are. But you should've told me about your parents."

"And have you throw me off the case for personal interest? Or worse, look at me like you are right now. I don't need your pity, Agent Shepard."

Jake cursed under his breath as Dana stormed past him and down the stairs. He caught up to her in the rain. He tapped the key fob and unlocked the doors to the SUV so they could escape the downpour, but Dana didn't get in. Instead, she turned to face him, the rain streaming down her face like tears. Her chest heaved with emotion as she raised her voice to be heard over the storm. "You came to me. You're the one who brought this nightmare back to life for me. Don't take me off the case. My parents deserve justice. *I* deserve justice."

"Justice isn't guaranteed, Dana. And it won't take away the pain."

"I know that. But I have to try. I have to know why they were taken from me. They were victims, Jake. I've never been this close to getting the answers I've spent my life searching for. I can't stop now. I need to see this through."

The rain might've been masking her tears, but there was no hiding the emotion in her voice. Jake recognized it; that need to make things right. He felt it every day as he tried to square the debt Ramirez paid. How could he deny her a chance at finding truth and absolution, when those were the things that had made him take this job in the first place?

His fingers ached to reach out to her, to smooth back the wet hair lashing her pale cheeks and trace her trembling lips. He wanted to show her he understood, but the walls that took him years to build couldn't be broken so easily. The best he could do was reach past her to open the passenger side door. "If we do this, we do it together. That means no more secrets."

Dana blinked at him, her lashes tangled and wet. "What do you want to know?"

"Everything."

Her throat bobbed as she swallowed thickly. "That's fair."

"Let's get to the hotel and dry off. Then you can start at the beginning."

She nodded and climbed into the SUV. Jake closed the door behind her and walked around to the driver's side. Inside, the silence was stifling, even with the sound of rain pelting the vehicle. He could feel Dana's dark eyes searching him.

Jake started the engine and glanced over at her before putting it in drive. "Don't make me regret this."

Her hand reached out and squeezed his. "You won't. I promise."

Jake's pulse quickened at her touch. He quickly broke contact and pulled out of the parking lot. Driving occupied his mind, but his thoughts kept wandering back to Dana. Though he believed her, that familiar dread began to coil in Jake's gut. Dana might be getting closer to the answers she needed, but Jake felt he too was getting closer to something—something he wanted to avoid.

34

Dana was towel-drying her hair when she heard a knock at her hotel room door. A quick glance through the peephole showed a freshly showered Agent Shepard. She opened the door and his clean scent followed him in. The appealing fragrance of his cologne mingled with something else. That's when she noticed the takeout bag in his hand.

"I ordered some dinner. Hope you don't mind."

"No. I'm starving."

He set the white plastic bag on the large desk and went about unpacking it. The sweet aroma of jasmine rice and curry filled the room. Dana eagerly took the container Shepard offered. Her lips twitched into a grin when she opened it. Red curry with vegetables. He'd remembered she was a vegetarian.

She sat cross-legged on the bed in her oversized Georgetown sweat-shirt and leggings, while Shepard turned the desk chair around to face her. They might look like two friends enjoying a casual meal, but Dana hadn't missed the appearance of Shepard's notebook. She owed him answers.

Letting herself enjoy a few bites of her meal before she began, Dana contemplated what to tell the hardened FBI agent who sat across from her. She intended to tell him everything, just as she'd promised, but she didn't know where to start. Her parents' murder had become a part of her. It'd been her sole focus for so long it was hard to separate it from her own life now—not that she had much of one. But that was what happened when you dedicated your existence to vengeance.

Again, Dana found herself wondering if she'd always been on a crash course with this destiny. It was becoming clearer by the day that she belonged here, working with Shepard and the FBI. She'd hoped science would help her track a killer, but maybe it took working with a trained killer to catch one.

The thought staunched her appetite. Dana put her chopsticks down and took a sip of water. When she set the bottle down, Shepard's eyes were on her.

"I guess now is as good a time as any to start." Dana sighed and uncrossed her legs. Fidgeting with a loose thread on the white comforter, she began. "I was thirteen when my parents went missing."

"Missing? Why do you say that?"

"Because that's what they were. For a while anyway. They left me with my grandparents in West Virginia while they went on vacation. They were supposed to be in North Carolina, finally taking a real honeymoon. My mom wanted to see the ocean." Dana had to stop to suck in a breath and blink away the stinging in her eyes. "Sorry."

"You don't need to apologize."

"I know, I just hate feeling so ... weak."

"You're not weak. You're human."

She lifted her head, her gaze meeting Shepard's. His blue eyes held hers. Beneath his stormy expression she saw understanding, and it gave her the strength to keep going.

"My parents told me they were going to Hilton Head. When they didn't come home, that's where the police started looking. It was weeks before the John and Jane Doe found in that crappy Maryland hotel were identified as my parents."

Jake frowned. "I read your parents' file. The MOs are slightly different."

Dana's chest tightened. "You have their case file?"

"Cramer shared some of the digitized documents with me before I left. They were encrypted. I no longer have access."

"I've been trying to get access to it for years."

"You haven't seen their crime scene photos?"

She shook her head. "Not officially."

"Then how did you know the scenes were similar?"

"A newspaper leaked two photos when my parents were identified."

"Do you still have them?"

She nodded. "At my office. But I've memorized them by now." Dana looked down at her hands. "That sort of thing sticks with you."

Shepard frowned. "I still find it odd that our unsub changed his MO. The wallets were left at all the current crime scenes with the victims, making them easy to ID. Your parents' were not."

"I thought about that," Dana replied. "It's been almost twenty years. Maybe the killer has evolved. Or maybe the current victims were random, and my parents weren't."

Shepard nodded and scribbled something in his notebook.

"Anyway," Dana continued, "my parents' death was ruled a murder-suicide."

"Why?"

"Because there was no murder weapon, no signs of struggle, drugs or anything that led the police to suspect foul play."

"Except the pentagram and empty poison vials."

Dana nodded. "But that only made the suicide theory stronger. I overheard my grandparents talking to the police officer who came to their house. They said it was just a satanic ritual gone wrong."

"Were your parents into that kind of stuff?"

"No. My mother was a high school math teacher, and my father was a bank manager."

"Is it possible his job at the bank was the reason he was targeted?"

Dana shook her head. "I looked into that. It was a small-town bank in West Virginia, and there were never any insurance claims or other inconsistencies that would make me believe so."

"What was the name of the bank?" Shepard scribbled down her answer. "When did you look into this?"

"When I was fifteen, but I followed up annually for ten years." Shepard's gaze lifted to hers. "I told you. I've dedicated my entire life to this. I intend to see this through."

"Have you explored the possibility that maybe they were involved in this satanic church we're investigating?"

"They weren't."

"Just because you don't want them to be—"

"That's not it," she interrupted. "They loved each other. They loved me."

"Love can make people irrational, unpredictable."

"You don't understand." Dana went on to tell him about her parents' love story. How they met and fell in love, their whirlwind marriage and her welcomed arrival. "Do they sound like the kind of people who would just give that all up?"

"No. I'll admit it doesn't fit. But Dana, that's not proof that they weren't involved in things you weren't aware of. In all these cases, murder-suicide could be a logical answer."

"It's not."

"We have to explore all options. Didn't you tell me that's what science is all about?"

Dana cocked her head. "When did you decide occult studies was a science?"

Shepard's mouth twitched into a tight grin. "Let's just stick to the facts. We have no suspects. No witnesses of any other person in the hotel rooms with our victims. No foul play. No signs of a struggle. We need to be prepared for what we might find at the church tomorrow."

"You think the victims were members? That they chose this kind of death?"

"It's a possibility you should prepare for."

Dana's heart stopped. When it picked up its rhythm again, it was at a much faster pace. She was lightheaded again. This couldn't be true. If Shepard was right, if her parents had chosen this path, it meant she'd wasted her life studying death.

Her heart pounded hard, drowning out reason as her mind desperately tried to grasp at straws.

"Hey." Shepard's voice cut through her panic. "Take a breath." He moved next to her, his wide hand on her back. "Put your head between your knees and breathe."

She felt the bed dip under his weight as she complied. His hand stayed on her back, rubbing slow circles until her breathing steadied.

Dana's cheeks heated with embarrassment when she sat up. "I'm sorry."

"It's only natural to feel the way you do."

"How would you know how I feel?"

"Betrayed. Alone. Lost." Jake's hand was still on her lower back, offering way too much comfort.

Dana stood, instantly cold without the warmth of his touch. "I told you, I don't like it when you profile me."

Jake sighed and moved back to the desk chair. He picked up his notebook and surprised her by snapping it closed.

"Are we done?" she asked.

"For now."

"No. I can keep going. You don't have to take it easy on me."

"Trust me, I'm not. You're tougher than some men I've put through interrogation training."

Dana deflated, taking a seat back on the bed. It wasn't fair that she was being so defensive. Jake was just doing his job. "I wish I could say I felt tough right now, but I just feel ..."

"Defeated?" he offered.

She nodded. "My life hasn't been easy. But I guess I always thought the choices I made would be worth it in the end."

35

Jake knew Dana was being modest when she said her life hadn't been easy. He'd done a deep dive into her history after talking to Cramer. He knew her grandparents had been ill for a long time, passing away when she was seventeen. That was a whole lot of death for someone to deal with at such a young age. It almost justified her field of study.

He'd also learned that rather than go into the system, Dana had emancipated herself shortly after her grandparents' death. After that, she'd lived a quiet life and focused on academics. She received a scholarship to Georgetown and excelled from there. Everything she'd accomplished, she'd done on her own. He understood that, respected it even. He also knew how hard it was to be alone in the world.

The fact that she didn't elaborate on how isolated her life had been only spoke to her strength. Her parents' death had altered her life's trajectory. Jake knew all too well what that was like. He wouldn't be in the FBI if it weren't for what happened in Ghazni.

"You're doing it again."

Jake looked up to see Dana studying him. "Doing what?"

"Chewing the inside of your cheek. You do it when you're working through something."

"It's nothing."

"Is it your friend? Ramirez?"

Dana's warm brown eyes were so inviting the truth slipped right out of him. "Yeah." He tore his gaze away. Standing, he walked to the window. "The rain always makes me think of him." Jake huffed a laugh. "He loved it. I've never met anyone who got so excited about the rain."

"The snow always makes me think of my parents. My mom loved it. They would both call in sick and take the whole day off so we could make waffles and go sledding on the first snowfall."

The fondness in Dana's voice only made Jake's heart ache more. "I don't think Danny ever saw the snow."

"When it snows, I always think it means my parents are looking down on me, kind of like guardian angels watching over me."

Jake turned to face her. "You don't actually believe that, do you?"

"Why not?"

"After all the horrible evil you study, you still believe there's that kind of goodness in the world?"

"You know what I've learned studying death? The thing we fear most isn't death, it's the finality of being alone. But for every story of hell, there's one of heaven. For every culture's devil, an angel exists to watch over us, and guide us through the evil. That's what I cling to when I feel my parents' loss the most. I let myself believe they're somewhere, watching, guiding, guarding me with their love, just like they would if they were standing right here next to me." Dana stood up and crossed the room, taking his hand. "It can be the same with you and Danny, if you let it."

Jake swallowed the lump in his throat, pushing thoughts of Ramirez and Dana's parents from his mind. As comforting as Dana's ideals were, Jake preferred to focus on the tangible, like the extraordinary woman standing in front of him. "I meant what I said before. If we're going to do this, we do it together."

"I know."

"If this is too much for you, I need to know now."

"I already told you it's not."

"All right. I won't ask again." He slipped his hand from hers and walked back to the desk to pack up his food.

"Are you leaving?"

"Do you want me to stay?"

Her cheeks flushed, but she shook her head.

"Then I think I'll call it a night. Unless you feel like flipping through murder books."

"Do you think that will help?"

Jake paused, looking up at her intense gaze. "That was a joke, Doc."

"Oh."

Seeing the desperation in her brown eyes put another chink in his armor. Perhaps he shouldn't leave her alone. "Maybe it could help."

"No, that's okay. I know the scenes inside out by now."

"I don't mind giving them another look with you. You were just at your parents' crime scene for the first time. You could've picked up on something new."

Dana's eyes widened. "You have my parents' murder book?"

"No. I put in a request, but since it's a cold case, it wasn't readily available. I just saw the few things Cramer shared with me."

"Right." The disappointment in her voice was clear.

"It should be on my desk when we get back to DC. I can see about getting you access to it if you'd like."

"Thank you."

Nodding, Jake walked toward the door. Something made him pause and turn back. Dana was still sitting on the bed, looking small and helpless, though he knew better than to tell her that. He'd meant it when he'd said her will was stronger than some of the men he'd trained.

Jake knew Dana could take care of herself, but that didn't stop him from worrying about her. And it didn't stop the dread from taking up more space in his gut. He couldn't shake the feeling that the victims weren't random. And now that he knew Dana's parents had been targeted, it was possible she was a target.

Working this case with him only increased those odds.

Jake knew he wouldn't forgive himself if he didn't warn her. "Don't take this the wrong way, but I'd feel better if we shared a room tonight."

Dana stood, eyes incredulous. Before she could bite his head off, Jake lifted his hands in surrender. "Just for your protection. I'd sleep on the floor, of course."

"Yes, you would, but it's not necessary. I'll be fine in my own room."

"For your sake, I hope you're right."

"What does that mean?"

"I've seen this before. Serial killers go dormant for decades and then something triggers the urge to kill again. The temptation to go after the same type of victim is too much to ignore. That makes you an aphrodisiac to this guy."

"You're sure it's a man?"

"More than eighty percent of serial murderers are male."

Satisfied by the statistic, she mulled it over. "The only similarities in the victims are that they were all in committed relationships. Lucky for me, I'm not."

Jake heard Claire's voice in his head. *Know when to pick your battles.* "Fine. But make sure you lock the door behind me. Use the security bolt too."

Dana followed him to the door. "Always do."

He gave her one last look, his fingers aching to reach out and hold onto her. He wanted to protect her from the cruelness of the world. But one thing life had taught him was that there were some forces of nature even he couldn't fight.

As the door shut behind him, he felt the fissures in his armor fusing back together. It was better that way. Letting Dana in would be a mistake, and mistakes were deadly in his business.

36

Thunder startled Dana awake.

Disoriented, it took her a moment to get her bearings. Lightning flashed, lighting up her hotel room. When she'd crawled under the covers, she'd thought the storm was over, but it must've started up again.

She sat up in bed, surprised that she'd actually slept sound enough to feel so groggy. She'd tossed and turned for hours after Shepard left, unable to get his words out of her head. The bedside clock read 4:11 AM, its bright red numbers washing the walls with an eerie glow in the darkness.

Untangling herself from her sheets, Dana hung her feet over the side of the bed and reached for her water on the nightstand. The bottle was empty. Parched, she stood and padded barefoot to the bathroom. The cold tile floor woke her further, dragging the cobwebs of sleep from her mind as she turned on the faucet to refill her water bottle. A scraping sound made her pause. She turned the water off and listened.

Shepard's words had wormed their way into her mind and were now playing tricks on her. She was not a target in this case. In a world with seven billion people, the odds of this killer coming after her were insurmountable. Her analytical mind argued against that blind logic.

She knew Shepard wouldn't be worried without reason. There were statistics to support his theory, but she didn't want to know them. Not if she ever hoped to get any sleep.

Turning the faucet back on, she finished filling her water bottle and returned to the bedroom. Before climbing into bed, her eyes darted to the locked door, just to appease her paranoia. And that's when she saw it. The security bolt. It was no longer latched.

A split second of panic was all she was afforded before the shadow near the curtain came alive. That split second gave her the advantage she needed. When the large man in a ski mask lunged for her, Dana was ready. Her fight-or-flight default had always been fight, and after the crash course of real world combat she'd just been through with Barnes, she was ready to redeem herself.

Refusing to be an easy target, Dana struck fast.

Her first kick landing true, her second taking him down. Not wanting to give up her gain, she slammed a knee into her attacker's back, using her full weight to keep him down, but he wasn't having it. The man scrambled for purchase, his arms and legs flailing as he tried to buck Dana off his back.

She needed something to restrain him.

Scanning the dark room, there weren't many options within reach. The lamp would have to do. Dana lunged for it, yanking it off the nightstand and toward her attacker's head in one powerful arc. Moments before the ceramic base made impact, the man rolled.

The sounds of shattering pottery rose above their struggle as the storm raged on, drowning out any hope that Shepard would hear the melee and come to her rescue.

No, Dana would have to do this herself; like everything else in her life.

She grabbed the base of the smashed lamp, clutching the power cord between her fists, her self-defense instructor's voice loud and clear in her mind. *Anything can be a weapon.*

The problem was, Dana's attacker knew this, too. And he'd come prepared.

As she rushed toward him with the cord, he pulled his own weapon and it was more deadly. Dana stopped in her tracks, the metallic gleam of the taser warning her not to get too close. It looked menacing as a flash of lightning lit the room.

The man wielded it toward her.

Images of what this monster could do to her if he rendered her unconscious flipped through Dana's mind like a horror movie. Keeping her distance, she did her best to study him as they made a slow waltz around the room. All the while Dana was committing every detail of her attacker to memory.

She was no match for a taser.

His weapon was a game changer, shifting the advantage back to him. Now, her only chance of self-preservation was escape. But she was going to take all the details of this masked man with her if she got the chance to run.

He was tall, approximately 6'3", broad shouldered, probably weighed two-twenty, and he was smart. He was wearing gloves and a full mask. His dark clothing was nondescript and covered all his skin. Dana wished she could hear his voice. Height and weight wouldn't be enough to go on.

"What do you want?" she yelled, continuing to keep her distance as she tried to edge her way toward the door.

The man said nothing, but he read her move, countering it with his own. He stood with his back to the door, blocking her only escape.

"Are you here because of the Romeo and Juliet murders?"

No response.

Dana's lips trembled. "Did ... did you do it? Did you kill my parents?"

She swore she saw his lips twitch beneath the mask.

Was that a smile?

There was no way of knowing. No way of finding out the truth, unless ... If she sacrificed herself, if she let him take her, then maybe she'd get to the bottom of this. Of course, there was no guarantee, and even if she found what she was looking for, there was little chance she'd be able to do anything with it.

Death tended to silence the truth. But did she care?

Dana wanted answers more than anything.

She'd always known there would be a price to pay. Maybe this man was finally here to collect. The only question that remained was whether she was willing to go all in.

She knew her answer. And it made her glad she hadn't let Jake share her room tonight. This man was here for Dana. There was no reason to make Jake a target, too. She refused to drag him any further into this mess. That's why she didn't call out to him. She wouldn't be the reason he died.

She squared her shoulders and spoke clearly. "If you tell me the truth, I'll go with you."

The masked man seemed to ponder her offer. Was she really doing this? Willingly submitting to the man who may have killed her parents? Before Dana had time to let her decision sink in, it was taken off the table. The masked man made his move, but so did someone else.

The door to Dana's room splintered open and Agent Shepard burst in, gun drawn. "Freeze, FBI!"

The commotion was enough to distract Dana's attacker. He stopped his advance on her and changed direction with astonishing speed.

"I said freeze!" Shepard shouted, widening his stance as he took aim, but the man didn't stop. He barreled into Shepard sending them both tumbling into the hall.

Dana raced after them, her eyes meeting Shepard's for a fraction of a second before the masked man jammed the taser into Shepard's torso, holding it there as an agonizing pain tore through the downed agent. Dana watched in horror as Shepard's body helplessly spasmed, the gun dropping from his hand. She had a split second to decide whether to go for the attacker's mask or Shepard's gun.

Instinct took over, and she body checked the man off Shepard and away from the gun. The move gave her the time she needed to recover the gun, but it also gave the masked man time to get away. He was on his feet, his long legs eating up the hallway when Dana brought the gun eye level to take aim. She had him in her sights. There was no way she didn't take the shot.

Her heart hammered as she squeezed the trigger. Unprepared for the kickback, her shot went high. The next two were even worse. Plaster dust rained down from the ceiling as the man rocketed his way through the metal exit door to the stairwell. A quick glance back at Shepard's rising chest told Dana he'd pull through. It was the only go ahead she needed to take off down the hall.

Racing after her assailant, Dana burst through the cold metal door, gun still drawn. She had no idea how many bullets she had left, but she planned to use every last one if that's what it took to bring this guy down.

Glancing between the three flights of railings, Dana caught a dark blur and fired. The shot ricocheted off the concrete steps, sparking as it missed her intended target.

Dana kept moving.

She raced down the stairs, her heart sinking when she heard another exit door fall shut. The sound echoed through the stairwell with the finality of a tomb. In her heart, she knew she'd lost him—her only chance at finding out who killed her parents—but she couldn't convince the rest of her to stop moving.

Panting, Dana pushed the emergency exit door open and stumbled out into the night. The pounding rain cooled her flesh, but it brought her no relief. Just like she'd expected, all traces of the masked man were gone. She stared into the empty darkness as disappointment brought her to her knees.

37

"No, I told you, Shepard, I'm done. Just take me off the case."

Jake stood in Dana's hotel room, watching her pack. Her hair was still wet, but at least she'd stopped shivering. He was pissed as hell and doing his best to hold it all inside. Now that he knew she was okay, he wanted to throttle her for taking on their attacker on her own.

He'd found her outside, crumpled on her knees and trembling almost as violently as he'd been from the taser. Fearing the worst, he'd started checking her for injuries. That's when she'd surprised the hell out of him by standing up, calmly handing him back his gun and walking back into the hotel without saying a word.

That had only infuriated him more. He knew his anger was misguided, but he was worried about her. They were supposed to be partners. She should've called out to him the moment that asshole broke into her room, not tried to handle it on her own. He was a part of this, whether she liked it or not. Jake had half a mind to tell her that right now, but he had a feeling it would fall on deaf ears. Dana was spiraling, and he didn't want to make things worse.

"Dana, you're shaken. It's understandable. You don't need to make any decisions right now."

"But I have. I've decided I'm done with this investigation." She continued angrily throwing things into her suitcase on the bed. "You were right from the beginning. I have no business being in the field. I never should've agreed to take this on. My personal interest is a liability."

"I don't agree."

"Well, you should. I've done nothing but screw everything up."

Jake sighed, ignoring his pounding headache as he bided his time. He'd been waiting for Dana to crack, and she was almost there. She'd held it together all night, or morning rather.

Dana answered his questions and the local PD's when they showed up to take her statement. But even the most seasoned agents could break under this kind of pressure, and Dana wasn't even an agent. She was a librarian, for Christ's sake.

Jake noted the way her hands began trembling as she tried to zip her suitcase shut. With the haphazard way she'd thrown her things inside, it had no chance of closing. Her shaking hands only made the task even more impossible. With the zipper jammed and the suitcase only halfway closed, Dana gave up, shoving it off the bed and onto the floor with a scream of frustration.

That final defeat did her in. Her dam burst. When Jake saw the first tear trickle down her cheek, he moved around the bed and pulled Dana to his chest, holding her even when she resisted. Her arms were tucked in tight, her elbow pressing against the sore spot on his abdomen courtesy of the taser, but Jake forced himself not to wince. Dana needed to let the traumatic events of tonight out now or they'd come out some other harmful way later.

Relief spread through him like a nip of bourbon when Dana finally gave in. Her arms relaxed to her sides as the tears kept coming. Her hands fisted his shirt as Dana let him hold her while she sobbed into his chest. Jake tucked her head beneath his chin, noting how fragile she felt. In a morbid way, it was a relief to him to know she could break. It made her feel more real, more like him.

Jake pushed the errant thought away. He stroked his hand down Dana's wet hair as she gasped and trembled in his arms. It was hard for him to believe she'd fended off an attacker, saved his ass, and then chased the perp down like Robocop.

Robocop with bad aim . . . but still.

"I lost him," she sobbed. "He showed up at my door, and I let him go."

"He showed up once, he'll show up again."

Dana leaned back just enough to look up at him, her big brown eyes spearing him. "You don't know that."

He shrugged. "No, but I have a pretty good hunch. And I'm usually right."

Jake meant to lighten the mood, but he could see Dana took his words to heart.

She pulled away from him. "I should've listened to you."

"You couldn't have known this would happen."

"You knew."

"Not definitively."

"If I'd listened to you, we could've caught him."

"Not necessarily." Jake knew how badly things could've gone. "We're lucky to both be standing right now. Speaking of, I think I need to take you to the shooting range when we get back to DC."

Dana crossed her arms. "I meant it, Jake. You're not going to change my mind. I'm done with this case. It's time I move on with my life."

Jake hid his grin. She wasn't done the same way he wasn't done. People like them, they couldn't walk away from unfinished business. But some things were better left unsaid. "Whatever you think is best." Jake leaned down and finished zipping her suitcase before standing it up and grabbing the handle. "You ready to head back to the city?"

Dana nodded. Halfway to the door, Jake felt her hand on his forearm. He paused, looking back. Her gaze was full of sorrow. "I'm sorry."

"For what?"

"For letting you down."

"You didn't."

"But I did. And when he kills again, it'll be my fault."

Jake let go of the suitcase and turned to face her. Without thinking, he took her face in his hands. "Dana, if he kills again, it's on him. Do you understand? He's the bad guy in this, not us. We do the best we can to stop this kind of violence, to protect people, but we're human. Some things aren't up to us."

"I know. That's the part I hate most."

"Me too."

"How do you keep doing this?"

"It's the job. I do what I can. And what I can't ... well I pray there's a special kind of hell reserved for the monsters who escape justice in this life."

Dana's shallow inhale reminded Jake just how close they were, her full lips a breath away from his. He let go before he did something stupid. "Come on. We need to leave now if we don't want to be stuck in DC traffic."

38

Two days later Dana sat outside SSA Cramer's office, waiting to be summoned inside. She didn't care how much the relentless FBI agent called her, she was not changing her mind about working the Romeo and Juliet case, and she was here to tell him so to his face.

Apparently, Jake had gone to bat for her, telling Cramer he'd been mistaken to think she was involved in the case and now the two-faced agent was begging her to stay on.

That wasn't going to happen. The only reason she'd showed up today was to tell Cramer where he could shove it.

Dana's gaze moved around the bland space, taking in the generic artwork and harsh lights. It was strange how familiar the J. Edgar Hoover Building had become to her in such a short time. So was the fact that she suspected she was going to miss her time with the FBI, or perhaps just one agent in particular.

She hadn't seen Jake since they returned from Maryland. He'd called twice to check in on her and let her know he was still following up on getting her access to her parents' old case file. She wasn't sure it would give her the peace of mind or closure she'd hoped for, but at this point, she was beginning to think such things didn't exist. At least not for people like her.

The deep blue door to Cramer's office opened, and he poked his head out. Spotting her, the aging agent smiled. "Dr. Gray, sorry to keep you waiting."

Dana stood and walked toward him, but he held up his hand. "Actually, I was thinking we could have this discussion somewhere else." He closed the door behind him, jacket in hand. "I'm starving. Mind making this a lunch meeting?"

Dana fell into step with him. "What we have to discuss won't take that long."

Cramer grinned. "I see why Jake thinks you'd make a hell of an agent. You've got some fight in ya."

His words nearly caused her to stumble. "He said that?"

"Sure did. He had quite a few compliments about your actions."

"Like what?"

Cramer winked. "I'll tell you all about it over lunch."

"You haven't touched your salad," Cramer commented, wiping the burger grease from his mouth with a cloth napkin.

"I'm not hungry." It wasn't true, but everything about the smug agent was rubbing Dana the wrong way, including watching him tear into his undercooked meat.

There was something unnerving about the man. His unwavering attention made her feel vulnerable. The posh DC café on Ninth was a public enough place, and the outdoor patio they dined on was packed with patrons enjoying their meals, but none of it put Dana at ease. She couldn't shake the unease that surrounded her under Cramer's scrutiny.

"Suit yourself." He pulled out a pack of Kents, the cigarette already in his mouth before he mumbled, "You mind?"

She shook her head. She wasn't a fan of cigarette smoke, but anything to move this meeting along. "What else did Shepard say about me?" she asked impatiently.

"That you're the key to blowing this case wide open."

"I disagree, and I already told him I'm no longer interested in working on this investigation."

"Dana, may I call you Dana?"

She nodded, begrudgingly, certain Cramer was using some kind of FBI intimidation strategy.

"I completely understand where you're coming from, Dana. What you went through in Vegas and then being attacked in Maryland, it would scare anyone."

"I'm not scared."

"Then what's keeping you from helping us nail this bastard? Jake tells me how close you got at the hotel. And there's some church he wants to go back to investigate?"

"That's why we went up to Maryland in the first place."

Cramer nodded. "I know. That and to see if you could be trusted."

Pushing her chair back, Dana dropped her napkin onto the table. "I don't need to justify myself to you. I've done nothing wrong, and now I'd like to forget about all of this and get on with my life."

Cramer stood quickly, blocking her path. "Dana, wait! Please, sit down and let me explain."

There was a hardness to his voice she didn't like. She crossed her arms, unwilling to let this man bully her.

Cramer exhaled a puff of smoke before stubbing out his cigarette with his shoe. "Look Dana, I brought you out here because this is something I don't do often."

"What's that?"

"Apologize. I was wrong to accuse you of being involved. After what happened in Maryland, Jake vouched for you, and that's good enough for me. I trust that man with my life. He's the closest thing to family I've got left."

"Good for you, but I don't understand what any of this has to do with me."

Cramer gestured for her to take a seat. Relenting, she sat, and he joined her. "I don't ask this favor lightly or for myself, but for Jake. I'd hate for anything to happen to him."

"What do you mean? Has something happened?"

"Not yet, but that's why I'm asking you to stick this thing out. I know Jake. He'll see this through even if it kills him."

"You think it'll come to that?"

"I don't know, but I do think he has a better chance with you by his side. I'm not sure he'll see this monster coming on his own."

It wasn't fair. Cramer was preying on Dana's heartstrings and he knew it. He had her on the fence, and she hated him for it.

Jake's blue eyes haunted her memories; his warm arms around her, his kind reassurances, his patience, his strength. Even though they'd only known each other a short while, Jake had been there for Dana countless times when she needed him. Did she owe him this? To stay the course?

No. She may have let herself lean on Agent Shepard, but it had been his choice to hold her up. Dana shook her head, making up her mind. "I'm sorry, Agent Cramer. I'm not changing my mind. This isn't what I want."

"What if I could give you something you *do* want?" That oily feeling slithered over her skin again as Cramer's grin widened. "I hear you're looking for your parents' case file?"

"Yes, I am, but Shepard said there's been some sort of freeze placed on the records."

"I can make a call, get that straightened out. Jake could have the files on his desk this afternoon."

"In exchange for me staying on the case?"

Cramer nodded. "Do we have an understanding?"

"How do I know you can get my parents' files?"

He laughed. "Who do you think issued the hold?"

Dana's mouth fell open, her protest drowned out by Cramer's incessant tsking. "This is DC. Leverage is a priceless commodity here. You'd do well to remember that."

"And you'd do well to remember that blackmail is a crime."

"Who said anything about blackmail? I'm simply inclined to do a favor for those who offer one in return." Cramer stood up. "Well, I'll let you think about it."

"I don't need to think about it."

"No?"

"Make the call now, and you have a deal."

Cramer smiled. "I knew I was right about you."

39

Everything about her meeting with Agent Cramer set Dana on edge.

She'd been determined to get on with her life, and she'd let the man bully her out of that freedom. Bully wasn't the right word; it was more like extort. She could tell he was a man used to getting what he wanted, and she hated that she'd given in to him.

When Dana woke up, she'd intended on going to the library to get back into her routine, but Cramer had just taken a battering ram to that idea.

She wouldn't be able to focus on anything until she saw her parents' files. And there was no way she was doing any work on this case until Cramer made good on his promise. So that left her with only one place to go.

Dana didn't bother to knock as she barged into Shepard's office. Stopping dead in her tracks, she instantly regretted that she'd let her anger override manners. Jake seemed just as shocked to be caught with his shirt unbuttoned. "Christ! Don't you knock?"

"Sorry," Dana mumbled, her eyes lingering on the bandage he was re-taping over the angry red signature marks the taser had left on his abdomen. A web of purple bruising peeked out from behind the bandage, marring his otherwise perfect muscles. "Are you okay?"

"I'm fine."

Hoping her cheeks weren't as red as they felt, Dana dragged her eyes away from Shepard as he buttoned up his shirt. She continued into his office, closing the door behind her.

Jake's brow furrowed. "What's up?"

"We need to talk."

"I DON'T UNDERSTAND." Shepard was pacing. "That doesn't sound like Cramer."

"I'm not making it up."

"I didn't say you were. I just don't understand why he'd do something like this, especially without telling me?"

Dana shrugged. She was getting impatient. She'd already relayed every detail of her conversation with Cramer for Shepard. She didn't see the point in spelling it out a second time. "Maybe he thought he was protecting you. He thinks of you as family."

"That's just an expression."

"He made it sound like more than that. His exact words were, 'He's the closest thing to family I've got left'."

Jake shook his head. "Cramer has a brother, but I get where he's coming from." He took a seat at his desk, his eyes landing on a photograph on the wall. "Cramer and I were both Army. It's brotherhood for life; stronger than family for some."

"For you?"

"There was a point when I thought so."

"And now?"

The buzz of Jake's receptionist interrupted his answer. "There's a courier here for you. Do you want me to sign for it?"

"Yes, please. And bring it in to me if you don't mind."

"Right away, sir."

Moments later Shepard's assistant, Margot, bustled in, a discolored white storage box in her hands. It was taped shut and marked classified. Jake took the box and thanked Margot. Dana stared at it, her stomach cramping as the woman left the room. This was it. The moment she'd been waiting for her entire life. The truth of what really happened to her parents was inside the yellowing box. Or at least she hoped it was.

Jake's voice was quiet when he spoke, as though he sensed the significance of the moment. "Are you ready?"

She shook her head.

"Do you need a moment?"

"I don't think I can do this here." She looked up at him. "Can we go to my office?"

Something like surprise flashed in his blue eyes as he caught her use of "my." "Sure. Wherever you feel comfortable."

Dana stood, approaching the box like it was a bomb. And rightly so, considering its contents could blow up her world.

Her hands gently traced the edges, leaving trails in the dust. She let her fingers slide into the indented handles, surprised by the lack of weight as she lifted the box. It seemed the lives of two people she cared so much about should've amounted to more. The space their loss had carved out in her heart was so vast there wasn't a box large enough to contain it.

"Dana, you don't have to do this right now if you don't want to."

"I want to. Besides, Cramer held up his end of this twisted bargain, it's time for me to do the same. Whatever's inside here might help us with our case."

"*Our* case? Does that mean you'll be needing this back?" Shepard asked, pulling an ID badge from his drawer.

A faint smile curved her lips. "For now."

40

Shepard stood at Dana's side, looking ready to swoop in if whatever she found inside the box was too much for her. It wouldn't be. She'd been preparing herself for this moment for nearly twenty years. Losing her parents at thirteen had hardened her. She'd taught herself not to need anyone back then, so she certainly didn't need anyone now. But she had to admit, it was nice knowing Jake was there.

Now that they were back in the familiar comfort of her office there was nothing left to do but face the truth. With the box clutched in her hands, Dana looked up at Jake.

"Do you want some privacy?" he asked. "Or should I stay?"

"Stay." Dana took one more steadying breath before lifting the lid, ready for answers; whatever they may be.

Sifting through all the information in her parents' case file felt like swimming through quicksand. There was so much information to digest, and each time Dana flipped to a new page in their murder book, she felt as though she was slicing a paper cut into her soul. The box may have been light, but Dana was sure she'd absorbed a thousand pounds of sorrow as she relived her parents' last moments.

She'd known what to expect but knowing and seeing were two different things. Dana was unprepared for how deeply the crime scene photos would affect her. They weren't more gruesome than the ones she'd seen since working this case with Shepard, but her connection to the victims made it impossible to look at things objectively, which was necessary if she hoped to find the monster that did this to her parents and get them the justice they deserved.

As difficult as it was to relive her parents' murder, she felt a strange sense of relief. Perhaps it was just that she'd no longer have to imagine how it ended with the evidence spread out before her. Now if only she could put the pieces together the right way, she could solve this puzzle once and for all.

"I don't see anything inconsistent with our current case," Jake said from beside her. "I think this could be our unsub's first scene."

Dana shook her head. "I disagree. I'd say it was at least his fifth."

"Why's that?"

"The pentagram." She pointed to a crime scene photo showing the satanic symbol painted on the familiar red and gold carpet. "All five points are filled in. If I'm correct about my theory of these killings correlating to the five sacrificial stages from the Pentanic Verses, my parents were the fifth and final in this series. Based on that theory, the crime scene we visited when we were called back from Vegas was the fourth of the current series because only four points were filled in. That means there's one more sacrifice still to come in order to complete the ritual."

"Is there a timeline for this type of thing?"

"Not that I'm aware of. The Pentacle Church isn't tied to lunar cycles or astrological events."

Jake scratched his head. "Maybe we need to come at this from a different angle."

"How so?"

"We need to find out what made the unsub go dormant for nearly twenty years."

"That's impossible without knowing who the killer is."

"That's why I think we need to go back to the church. It might give us a starting point. We can look at the members and cross reference the ones who've been with the church for over twenty years with any life altering events that might've triggered a psychotic break that sent them down this path again."

Dana nodded. "That seems like a good way to narrow down our suspect pool."

Jake's brow furrowed. "*Our* suspect pool? Does this mean you're officially my partner again?"

"I don't know, but I'm more convinced than ever that my parents' death wasn't a suicide. Ritualistic suicides exist, but not outside concentrated cult practices. In our current investigations, we've yet to find anything to connect the victims to each other, let alone a cult."

Jake grinned, not missing that she'd said *our* again. "What about the church?"

"My parents weren't secretly members of the Pentacle Church."

"How can you be sure?"

"I just am."

"Is that your scientific opinion?"

She knew he was being sarcastic, so she ignored the comment, but Jake wasn't deterred.

"I think we should make a trip back up to Maryland and cross reference our vics with the church's list of parishioners."

Shepard wasn't wrong. The church might help them make some connections or at the very least rule some out. But Dana couldn't shake the feeling that the answers they were looking for lay somewhere in her parents' file. She kept the thought to herself though, worried Shepard would question her objectiveness.

A shock of black hair poked into Dana's office. "Am I interrupting?" Claire asked.

Dana shook her head and waved her intern in. Claire had made herself scarce for the past few hours to give Dana some space to go through her parents' files. It made Dana appreciate the girl's considerate nature even more. But she was grateful for Claire's interruption. Dana needed a break. And it seemed Jake did too.

He stood up from the desk, stretching as he greeted Claire. "Hey, Elvira."

"Hey, Secret Agent Man."

Warmth spread through Dana watching their interaction. Claire had slowly found a way to thaw Jake's bristly exterior. Dana had a sneaking suspicion it was the takeout that won him over, but she'd never say so. It was good to see Claire opening up more.

When Claire ambled over, Jake grinned. "Bring us anything to eat?"

"That's why I'm here. I was just about to place an order. You guys want anything?"

"You are my takeout spirit animal," Jake teased.

Claire beamed at the praise. "Then I'll double my order." Her attention drifted to Dana. "Dr. Gray, can I get you anything?"

"No thank you. I'm not hungry."

Claire and Shepard exchanged a worried look.

"You doing okay with all of this?" Claire asked.

Her concern was endearing, but Dana had always played the parental-type figure in their relationship. She didn't see why the roles should reverse. Just because this case was about Dana's parents didn't mean she was suddenly infantile.

"I'm fine," she said, returning to the photograph she was studying.

In her peripheral, she saw Shepard motion Claire aside. "I'll make the food run if you stay here with Gray," he murmured.

"Sure thing."

Dana sighed. "You both know I can hear you, right?"

Ignoring her, Jake headed for the office door. "And add something to the order for Dr. Gray. She needs to eat."

Claire took up the chair Shepard had been occupying after calling in their takeout order. "It's sweet the way he looks after you."

Dana looked up. "I don't need looking after."

"I didn't say you did. I just said it's sweet." Claire rested her elbows on the desk and propped her chin in her hands wistfully. "I wouldn't tell him he couldn't put his boots under my bed."

The comment startled a laugh out of Dana. She wasn't used to her normally timid assistant being so bold. Jake was bringing her out of her shell. Dana wasn't sure she liked it. "This is an FBI investigation, Claire, not a place to pick up men."

"Oh swipe right while you have the chance. Shepard is a snack!"

"A what?"

Claire rolled her eyes. "I'm just saying you should live a little."

"I live plenty."

Claire shook her head. "No, you don't. Neither of us do. Our whole lives have been devoted to books and research. I don't regret that, but I won't let it mean I don't get to have a life. I mean, look at this." Claire pointed to the crime scene photos spread out across Dana's desk. "If this doesn't make you want to go out and live every moment before it's too late, nothing will."

The swirl of emotions in Claire's watery eyes made Dana's heart ache. Maybe Jake had been right to try to shield Claire from this case. It was affecting her more than Dana had expected. But then again, sometimes she was guilty of forgetting that Claire was only in her twenties and still naïve enough to believe the world wasn't a bleak and hopeless place.

Dana reached out and squeezed her intern's pale hand. "Claire, you're trembling."

She quickly pulled her hand away. "I'm fine. I just need a smoke."

"Claire, you know how I feel about those things."

"They're only cloves," she argued.

"Yes, but smoking ..." Dana's words trailed off as her thoughts snagged on a memory.

Several images snapped together in her mind at once, forming a clear picture. Dana gasped.

"Dr. Gray ..."

"Claire! You're a genius! The cigarettes! It's him!"

Now Dana was the one shaking as she dug through the files on her desk until she found the photograph she was looking for. There, in the corner near the hotel dresser, was a cigarette butt. A Kent cigarette butt.

Dana's mind snapped back to the night Shepard had brought her to the hotel room where her parents had been found. The dresser had cigarette burns in it. She thumbed through more photos of their crime scene until she located the dresser. It was one of the few items that was still the same in the room when she'd visited. And the burns were there in the photos!

Dana's mind skipped to one more memory, the last piece of the puzzle that made her heart gallop in her chest. Her, sitting across a bistro table from a smug FBI agent, who'd been unable to resist his crutch.

Nearly hyperventilating, she grappled for her phone and dialed Shepard's number. "Pick up, pick up, pick—"

"Shepard."

"Jake! It's him. It's Cramer!"

"What are you talking about?"

"Cramer is the killer!"

"Dana ..."

"No! I'm right about this. Just get back here and I'll show you."

41

Jake popped his last dumpling into his mouth and savored its tangy perfection before indulging Dana's most recent crazy theory.

He'd told her he wouldn't even entertain listening to her until she ate something.

Jake had never seen someone eat so fast. And as a man who'd spent the better part of his life in the military, that was saying something.

Dana sucked down her drunken noodles like a champ before launching into her campaign against Cramer.

Jake and Claire finished their meals in silence while Dana ranted on about his boss's guilt. Now that Jake had finished eating, he couldn't stall any longer. "Yes, that brand of cigarette is a match, but Cramer isn't the only one who smokes Kents."

"I know he's your friend and you don't want it to be him, but you can't ignore the evidence."

"Cramer being a fan of Kent cigarettes is hardly evidence."

"What about the fact that he fits the description of my attacker?" Dana argued. "Six-three, two-twenty."

Jake ran a hand down his face, trying to work some of his tension out. "Do you know how many people fit that description?"

"Jake, I know it's him! The entire time we were at lunch today something felt off. Like there was something familiar about him I couldn't place, but now I know why. He's the one who attacked me. He's the killer. I can feel it in my gut!"

"Why would he take you out to lunch and beg you to stay on the case if he was the one who attacked you?"

"I don't know. Maybe he likes to keep his enemies close."

"I'm telling you, I know this man. He's not our enemy."

"He's the one who said you needed me because you wouldn't see the monster coming. Cramer is in your blind spot, and he knows it."

"Okay, hypothetically, let's say you're right and Cramer's behind this whole thing. We need evidence. Actual concrete facts. Your gut isn't going to take down a highly respected FBI agent who also happens to be a decorated war hero."

Dana surprised him by agreeing. "You're right. So how do we get the evidence we need?"

Jake sank into the chair in Dana's office. "It's not that simple."

Dana dragged a chair up next to him. "It all fits, Jake. The initial profile was that the killer was someone with a possible military background and knowledge of police procedure. Cramer has both. You have to see that."

Jake pinched his brow. "Yes, but so do literally thousands of other FBI and CIA agents, not to mention all the other private security agencies in the city."

"But none of them have access to this case like Cramer does."

"That we know of," Jake argued. He didn't want Dana to be right. Thomas Cramer had been a mentor to Jake, someone he'd looked up to when he'd joined the Bureau. Someone he thought had his six. He'd never expect to be stabbed in the back by Cramer, but if Dana was correct, that's exactly what his boss had done.

She sighed. "I get it. It's hard for you to imagine someone you're close to could be involved, but you can't ignore the facts. Cramer is a trained and experienced killer. He's an authority figure who craves power and control, and if that's no longer being satisfied in his current position, he may be seeking it elsewhere."

"Craves power and control?" Anger surged hot under Jake's skin. "Is that your general opinion of people who dedicate their lives to serving this country?"

"Not at all. But think about it. Cramer has been pitting us against each other from the beginning. What if he only made you think I was a suspect, so you'd doubt me right now when I figured it out?"

"He's not that conniving."

"He was conniving enough to leverage my parents' cold case to keep me where he wanted me."

"That doesn't make any sense. If he's behind this, I don't get the logic in keeping you on the case. What's his endgame?"

"I think it's obvious."

Jake crossed his arms. "Humor me."

"I think you were right in Maryland. I'm a temptation to this unsub. He's been saving me for his last kill."

"There's one flaw in your theory."

"What's that?"

"You're the one who pointed out that this guy always kills in pairs, remember?"

"I'm aware."

"Then who's the other target?"

Dana's dark gaze was full of sympathy. Her eyes never left Jake's as she turned to her intern who was lurking in the corner. "Claire, what's the definition of partner?"

"Either of a pair of people engaged together in the same activity," she parroted.

Claire's words hit their mark, just as Dana had intended. She hadn't planned to make Jake feel like a complete fool, but the result was the same, nonetheless.

Jake's mind whirled as he tried to process this new information.

Standing, he began to pace.

He was conflicted. He didn't want to believe that his Army brother and mentor could be behind this, but Dana's argument was compelling. Cramer could've orchestrated this whole thing.

He'd been adamant that Dana be brought on to the case, and he broke protocol by insisting she stay on after he'd found out about her parents' murder. Jake knew Cramer to be a pretty relaxed supervisor, but he'd demanded to be kept in the loop with every detail and development discovered in this case.

At first Jake had attributed it to the media pressure, but now he wasn't so sure. He was starting to see everything in a new light after Dana's revelation.

All at once, the evidence added up. Doubt clicked into place, giving a voice to the dread that had been building inside Jake since this case started. If he was honest with himself, something had felt off since the first time he'd seen Cramer smoking at the crime scene.

Swearing under his breath, Jake took a seat before his legs gave out on him. He ran a hand through his hair in frustration, gripping the back of his neck as he came to terms with this new reality. "If you're right, and that's still a big *if*, we need to tread carefully."

"If I'm right, Cramer is going to kill again and we're the only ones who can stop him."

"Yeah," he laughed bitterly. "And if we don't, we're the ones who end up dead. He'll eliminate the only people who could possibly implicate him in the crimes." Jake almost admired the genius of it. *The perfect crime.*

"So what do we do?" Dana asked. "Is there some sort of internal affairs task force that can help?"

Jake shook his head. "The best thing to do is wait."

"Wait? For what? Cramer to kill us?"

"No. He's setting a trap. We have to let him spring it."

"Have you lost your mind?"

"It's the only way. We have to catch him in the act, or we don't have enough evidence on him."

"Okay, but we'll at least need back up."

"No. If Cramer's involved there's no telling how deep the deception runs. By bringing in other agents, we risk tipping him off. If we do this, we do it alone."

Jake would never ask anyone to put their life on the line, but that's what Dana would be doing here. He needed to make that clear to her and let her know she had an out if she wanted it. Jake didn't. If Cramer was their unsub, bringing him down had just become personal.

He stood, crossing the room to where Dana sat. He knelt in front of her, his hands squeezing her knees. "If we do this, it's a risk. A big one. I would never ask you to put yourself in harm's way. God knows you've already suffered enough, but that's what this might come to. I need you to make a decision now so I can map out how this is going to go down. Are you in or out?"

She responded without hesitation. "This guy killed my parents. You know I'm in."

Jake fought against the conflicting emotions Dana's response filled him with. After all she'd been through, he had an almost unreasonable desire to protect her. But he knew that was the last thing she wanted. And who was he to deny her the justice she'd spent her life searching for?

"All right." Jake stood, and so did Dana. "From here on out, it's just me and you."

"We've made it this far together."

Jake extended his hand and Dana shook it, offering him a surprising grin. The woman really was something else.

"Where do we go from here?" she asked.

Jake crossed his arms. "We don't have solid evidence yet, but I think I know where we can get some."

"Where?"

"Ohio."

42

"Can I help you?"

Jake groaned at the unwelcome intrusion, but turned on his charm like switching on a light bulb. "You know, I could use some help."

He jogged down Rycroft Cramer's front steps with an easy grin and extended his hand to the elderly man who'd just crossed the overgrown yard and strode up to the porch.

"John Kent," Jake said, slipping into the familiar alias he used in situations like these.

"Martin McNeely. I live next door."

"Nice to meet you, Martin. I was hoping to visit an old friend while I'm in town, but he doesn't appear to be home. I don't get up to Ohio too often. I guess I should've called."

The older man's wrinkles deepened as he frowned. "If you're here to see Richard Boyd, you're about four months too late."

Jake blinked in genuine confusion. Who was Richard Boyd? He was here to see Cramer's older brother.

Martin sighed, shoving his hands deep in his overall pockets. "I'm sorry to be the one to break it to ya, but Richard passed on a few months back."

Jake shook his head, wondering if he'd taken a wrong turn. He pulled out his phone to check the GPS. "This is Willet Drive, right?"

"Sure is."

"Maybe I got the wrong address."

Martin shrugged. "I've lived here for twenty-odd years. Richard's owned the house next to me for the past ten or so."

The hairs on the back of Jake's neck began to rise. Something wasn't right. He was here to see Rycroft, but the neighbor was talking about someone named Richard. Not one to ignore his gut, Jake swiped through the photos on his phone. Finding what he was looking for, he held it up to Martin. "You sure we're talking about the same guy?"

"Yep. That's him. Poor SOB. Cancer got him. Fought it hard, but it's not a fair fight at his age. You two were close?"

"I was closer with his younger brother. I can't believe he didn't mention the cancer was back."

"Eh, Richard wasn't much of a talker. Kept to himself mostly."

"What about his brother? Was he here to help him at least?"

Martin shrugged again. "I never saw anyone at the house but ol' Richard. A few maintenance vans have been by lately, but that hasn't stopped the place from going to hell. It's turning into a real eyesore. Maybe you could talk to his brother about it."

"Absolutely," Jake said. "I wish I had a key. I could take a look around and make a list of what needs attention for him. He's pretty busy with work. I'm not sure when he'll have time to get up this way."

"Ya know what ..." Martin held up a finger and walked around the raised garden that showed off a harvest of dried weeds and broken terracotta pots. He picked up a small stone statue in the shape of an angel, snatching something from the dirt. "Whatta ya know? It's still here."

He walked back over to Jake and handed him a dirty and slightly rusted key. "Old homeowners kept it there. Not sure if Richard changed the locks, but it's worth a shot. I'd hate to see this place rot."

"I won't let that happen," Jake assured him, bounding up the steps. If the key didn't work, he'd pick the lock. But he couldn't do that with the nosy neighbor breathing down his neck.

He slipped the rusty metal into the keyhole, already thinking of a way to distract Martin, when he felt the lock tumble. Jake turned the knob and the old red door opened with a groan. Warm, stale air that smelled faintly of cigarettes wafted out onto the covered porch, stirring Jake's suspicion.

Something definitely wasn't right. He needed to get rid of Martin so he could take a look around. Turning back to the old man, he smiled. "It works. Thanks so much for your help." He held up his cell phone. "I'm gonna call his brother and see what we can do about the upkeep. Mind if I knock on your door when I'm done?" *Take the hint buddy.* Jake hated the idea of incapacitating the old-timer, but he'd do what needed to be done to get to the bottom of this.

Luckily, it didn't seem like Martin was going to make things more difficult.

The old man nodded. "Please do."

With a salute, Jake slipped inside and closed the door.

Relief from escaping the nosy neighbor was fleeting. Once inside Rycroft's house, Jake's skin began to tingle. The place felt *wrong*. There was no other way to describe it. Everything was in its place, but the home didn't feel lived in. It seemed like it was waiting for something, or someone.

Fractured ideas started to take shape in Jake's mind as he walked from room to room revisiting what he knew. Rycroft Cramer was using an alias. He may or may not be deceased. He'd have to quietly look into that to confirm Martin's story. Whoever lived here was or had been a serious smoker.

As far as Jake knew, Rycroft didn't smoke. He'd met the man at several DC functions and remembered how poor his health had been. He'd survived cancer twice—but perhaps not a third?

Either way, Rycroft was always on his younger brother to quit smoking. That told Jake that Cramer had most likely been visiting his brother's house recently. Perhaps to check on him while he'd been in poor health. Or was it to decompress from the heinous crimes he'd been committing in DC?

The neighbor didn't recall seeing Cramer visit, but that didn't surprise Jake. Cramer would've been careful, most likely coming in and out during the cover of night or in disguise. Perhaps he'd been the one driving the maintenance vans Martin saw? Jake had to consider that Cramer was also using an alias in Ohio. And that was probably the reason they wouldn't find Cramer's name associated with the church.

Jake couldn't wait to get back and have Dana cross reference Richard Boyd with the church's creepy congregation. But first he needed to do a more thorough search of the house. Slipping a pair of latex gloves from his pocket, Jake got down to business.

He worked the scene with the methodical precision befitting of the FBI. Moving room to room he cataloged what he found in his notebook. The single-story, brick ranch didn't take long to canvass. Two bedrooms with dated plaid wallpaper, one bathroom with tarnished brass fixtures, a small living room with worn leather furniture, a boring beige kitchen, and a bare mudroom and foyer.

Concluding his search of the first floor, Jake moved to the basement door. As he descended the stairs, his stomach twisted. One glance into the subterranean room told him why.

"Shit." Jake pulled his phone out of his pocket. He needed to get back to Dana.

43

Waiting was not Dana's strong suit. Jake had only been gone a little over twelve hours, and already she was climbing the walls.

She'd always loved the quiet of the library, but now it was enough to drive her mad. She needed something to silence her thoughts, and there was nothing on the underground floor that helped. She'd already been through the *Pentanic Verses* a million times, along with all the online church records she could get her hands on. There wasn't much to go on, and so far she hadn't found anything helpful. There were no records of a Thomas Cramer, Rycroft Cramer, or any Cramer for that matter being associated with the Pentacle Church.

Dana regretted giving Claire the day off. She needed a distraction. Sometimes, just knowing her quiet intern was sharing the same space was often enough to make Dana feel less alone. She considered calling Claire. Normally, the girl wasn't the chattiest, but given the right topic, she could talk to a housefly. But Dana didn't really want to talk about Egyptology or Thai cuisine. She wanted to talk to Jake. But he was off trying to track down Cramer's brother in Ohio.

Jake was convinced Rycroft Cramer could help shed some light on the situation, or at the very least talk some sense into his younger brother and get him to give up his murderous tendencies. Dana wasn't sure she agreed the brother would be of any help. Not having siblings of her own, she couldn't comprehend the true weight the bond carried, but Jake assured her it was worth pursuing. She didn't bring up the faulty logic in his theory. According to Jake, the Army should've made Cramer consider him a brother, but that hadn't stopped him from making Jake a target in whatever twisted game he was playing.

It was killing Dana to feel so in the dark. She chewed her thumbnail as she aimlessly paced the stacks, praying Jake knew what he was doing. The words he'd said to her in his office drifted back to her. *A bond stronger than family for some.*

If Cramer could turn on his Army brother, he could turn on anyone.

Dana was convinced he was a lost cause. He'd have to be to have done the horrible things she suspected. If she was right and Cramer truly was the Romeo and Juliet killer, that meant he'd killed eighteen people in cold blood, maybe more. And if she didn't do something about it, he'd kill again.

And this time, she was the one in his sights.

The thought was both comforting and sickening. On one hand, if she had to die so others didn't, it was a small price to pay. But there was no guarantee Cramer would go dormant for another twenty years. Plus, there was the fact that if she was at risk, so was Jake.

Dana might be okay giving up her own life for the greater good, but she'd never risk someone else's. Especially not Jake's. She didn't want to drag him deeper into this mess, but she didn't know what to do about it.

Time was running out. Dana could feel it, like sand slipping through an hourglass. The sound of her phone ringing startled her, but not more than the name she saw on the caller ID. She steadied herself and answered. "Hello?"

"Hello, Dr. Gray. I think we need to talk."

"So do I."

"Good. Meet me at our café on Ninth. One hour."

"Pick up, pick up, pick up."

When Shepard's phone went to voicemail for the fifth time, Dana gave up. Not being able to talk to Jake was making her anxious. And that was before she agreed to do something this stupid.

Sighing, Dana slipped her phone back into her purse. She'd known trying to reach Jake was a long shot. For their plan to work, he needed to go dark. That meant disabling his cellphone so he couldn't be traced to Ohio where he was secretly trying to track down Cramer's brother.

Jake told Cramer that he and Dana were in Maryland following up on the church lead again. But the fact that Cramer had called her to meet meant he must've been onto their ruse, even though she'd stayed out of sight just like Jake instructed. Dana had even gone as far as to sleep in her office to not blow their cover, but it'd apparently been unnecessary.

As usual, Cramer was one step ahead.

She hated this cat-and-mouse game they were playing. And now that Jake's plan had divided them, Dana couldn't help thinking Cramer had the upper hand.

If we do this, we do this together. Dana couldn't get Jake's words out of her head. He'd be pissed if she went to this meeting alone, but what choice did she have? If she didn't, Cramer might run, and her chance for vengeance would be lost.

There was no way to justify the absurdity of her plan. Any way she sliced it, Jake would be against the idea. She could almost hear his deep voice, telling her to *stand down* in that strangely appealing alpha way of his. She knew he was just trying to do his job and protect her, but Dana was never someone who wanted protection.

She wanted the truth ... and Cramer had it.

What did she care if she died? Hadn't this monster already taken her chance at a normal life when he killed her parents? Maybe her existence was all just borrowed time, counting down to the moment she'd been destined for—taking the life of the man who'd ruined hers.

44

As soon as his plane touched down on the Dulles tarmac, Jake had his phone out. He had a voicemail from Dana, but his service blinked in and out as he taxied. Frustration bubbled inside him as he waited to get out of the jammed signal area. Added after 9/11, he knew the safety precaution was a necessity at the highly targeted airport, but he was eager to speak to his partner.

A jolt of excitement rippled through him at the notion of having someone like Dana Gray as a partner. As much as he'd been against it in the beginning, he'd grown to enjoy working with her. *At least Cramer did one thing right*, Jake thought bitterly.

Without Dana, Jake never would've unraveled this mess. But now he was more convinced than ever that she was right about Cramer. Jake's quick trip to Ohio had revealed unexpected results. He was returning without Cramer's brother, but by no fault of his negotiation skills. But the trip hadn't been fruitless.

Jake used back channels to confirm the neighbor's story about Rycroft's death. Just like he'd said, it happened four months ago. Exactly the time the murders began.

That was a trigger if Jake had ever heard one.

And from what Jake saw inside the house, there was no doubt

Cramer's brother had been involved in some strange shit. Perhaps he'd even been the one to pull Cramer into the Pentacle Church. When Rycroft passed, Cramer might've felt compelled to carry on the messed-up family tradition.

Visiting Rycroft Cramer's last known address revealed a neglected home holding a treasure trove of condemning evidence. The pagan altar and pentagrams in Rycroft's basement looked like a scene out of one of Dana's ancient occult books. That, along with copies of the *Pentanic Verses* and other strange biblical writings, were all Jake would need for a warrant. There were dozens of undeveloped rolls of film. Jake didn't have to see what was on them to know what they were.

Trophies.

He'd bet money each one was from a victim. But the most damning evidence at the house were the cigarette butts. Dozens of them. All Kent.

He bagged a cigarette for evidence so he could get a DNA match. Otherwise, he left the scene undisturbed. Once they had Cramer in custody, he'd go back with a team to process everything.

The thought made his stomach twist.

After what Jake had seen and done during his time in the Army, he could almost understand it. How people could lose their faith and turn elsewhere looking for any form of redemption to cling to. For Cramer it turned out to be the Pentacle Church. His spiral into darkness must've been easy with his brother to guide him. Jake understood how it could happen, but that made it hurt worse. Because if it could happen to Cramer that meant it could happen to him.

Unless he could stop the darkness from swallowing him, too.

Dana popped into Jake's mind again. She was a bright spot in his life, and he didn't want to disappoint her. Whatever led Cramer down this path wasn't important. Jake went to Ohio to find answers, and what he found inside the basement was more than enough to make the Cramer brothers the prime suspects in the Romeo and Juliet murders.

There were still a lot of dots to connect, but the most important thing now was getting to Dana before Cramer did.

Jake hated not checking in with her when he was in Ohio, but it was too great a risk. One inkling of Jake being onto Cramer could spook him into the wind, or worse, accelerate his plan. And when plans were rushed, killers got sloppy. He wouldn't put Dana in more danger than she was already in.

Finally, Jake's plane arrived at the gate. The seatbelt sign turned off at the same time he got enough service to listen to his voicemail. Dana's voice greeted him on the other end. But the tone of her voice made his muscles coil with unease.

"Jake, it's me. I think he knows we're onto him. He asked me to meet him today. The café on Ninth. One hour from now. I know it's a risk. But not going is an even bigger one. I'm not letting him get away with this. I know you said we were in this together, but this part ... I think I need to do alone."

The recording ended, filling Jake's veins with ice. Badge in hand, he was on his feet, pushing through the log jammed aisle with only one thought. Get. To. Her. First.

45

The slimy way he grinned as Dana approached made her cringe. Everything about SSA Cramer had made her skin crawl the first time they met. This time was no exception. At least this time she knew why his presence made her hair stand on end. The man oozed malevolence, but she refused to let him see her sweat.

Dana knew this meeting was just as much about luring her into his trap as it was about her catching him. She planned to exude as much false confidence as possible to stall him and give Shepard a chance to get her message, but she was prepared to see this through, even without him. Cramer's end game didn't really matter to Dana. She'd come prepared to meet whatever end he had planned for her, as long as she got the truth first.

"Dana, thank you for joining me," Cramer said, standing in a pointless show of manners.

"You can cut the act. I know why I'm here."

His thick gray eyebrows rose with amusement, but he took a seat. "I do enjoy a woman who cuts to the chase."

"I don't see the point in wasting time."

"Neither do I."

"Then admit it."

"Admit what?"

"That you're the one behind this." She lowered her voice for the sake of the other patrons in the crowded café. "The Romeo and Juliet murders, my parents, attacking me in my hotel room. I know you're responsible."

"Do you now?"

"Yes. But what I want to know is why?"

He grinned. "I thought you might." But then he signaled to the waitress. "You'll get your answers," he said as the young brunette hurried over to take their order. "But first we're going to enjoy a meal."

"I'm not hungry," Dana hissed under her breath as the waitress awkwardly watched the exchange.

"Maybe not now, but for what I have planned, you'll need your strength." He gave the waitress his oily grin. "I'll have the softshell crab; she'll have the stuffed portabella."

The girl nodded and hurried away.

"This isn't a game, Cramer."

"I know that."

"Then tell me why you've done this."

"Are you sure you want to know? It might spoil your appetite."

"I told you, I'm not hungry. I just want the truth about my parents."

He made a tsking sound with his tongue that made her blood boil. "Let's not be too hasty," he warned. "Everyone deserves a last supper, Dana. James and Renee would've wanted that for you."

Her heart skipped a beat at the mention of her parents' names. Her throat was so dry that she had to take a sip of water before she could speak again. "So you admit it then? You did it? You killed them?"

"I thought you'd already condemned me?"

Dana's hands trembled so hard the condensation on her water glass made it nearly impossible to grip, but she forced herself to take another sip to cool the rage racing through her. The smug man across the table from her had killed her parents, and he was calmly gazing at her like this was a normal conversation to discuss over a meal.

Realization dawned on her. Cramer's decision to meet at the crowded café made sense. At first, it'd put her at ease, thinking he'd made a mistake bringing her to such a public place. But she now realized it was for his own protection. Because the rage boiling inside her made her want to leap across the table and strangle him with her bare hands.

But she couldn't do it. Not just because there would be too many witnesses, but because all the other victims' families deserved this opportunity too. To face the man who'd stolen something precious and irreplaceable from them; to take away his power.

Until this very moment, Dana hadn't known that was the thing she wanted most. To look him in the eye and tell him he didn't win. She'd come here thinking she was okay with dying, that her life had already ended because of what he'd taken from her, but she was dead wrong. Here, sitting across from this man who dealt in death, Dana had never felt more alive. She clung to it, letting her anger make her bold.

Dana willed a coolness into her voice. "You don't have much longer. You should confess and unburden yourself now while you have the chance."

"While I have the chance? Do you have plans for me, Dana?"

"Agent Shepard does."

Cramer chuckled. "Does he now?"

She pulled her cell phone from her purse, holding it up to show him the recording app that was still running. "Jake will be here any minute, and we have all the proof we need." She clicked stop on the recording. "Now's your chance. Tell me why you chose my parents."

"Not yet," he said, calmly. "But I can tell you, being chosen was the most interesting thing that ever happened in their dull little existence. That is, until you came along." Cramer reached across the table and took her hand. Dana tried to pull away, but his grip was strong. "What a pity. They fought so hard for you. But you'll be with them soon. I'll take you to them as soon as you're ready."

She yanked her hand away. "I'm not going anywhere with you!" She stood, almost stumbling into their waitress, sending the tray she'd been carrying flying. Dana's vision danced as she gripped the table to steady herself. She felt dizzy. Cramer's laughter came to her as if she were under water. She felt his arms move swiftly around her, his dry lips brushing against her ear as he spoke. "I'm sorry. I know you were expecting your white knight to come riding in to save you."

"Jake ..." A million questions raced through her foggy mind. *Where was he? Had he received her message? Would she ever see him again?*

"Don't worry," Cramer whispered, "his part in this isn't over. And neither is yours."

Another wave of wooziness washed over Dana and she realized too late she'd been drugged. Cramer forced her glass of water to her lips again. She was powerless to resist. A moment later, she couldn't even hold herself up. A crowd of onlookers gathered as Cramer gently lowered her to the ground. He spoke loudly. "Sweetheart? Did you take your insulin today?"

Dana tried to respond, but there was nothing she could do but lie still, her body fighting against the poison he'd laced her water with.

"Sweetheart," Cramer crooned. "It's okay. Take deep breaths. Everything's going to be all right now." She saw the flash of the syringe as Cramer flicked the tip of the needle before uncapping it. The man was an evil genius. He was drugging her right out in the open, and there wasn't a thing anyone would do to stop him. Not when he looked like a concerned father helping his diabetic daughter.

The last thing Dana felt was the tiny sting of the needle as more of the drug entered her system—nightshade—the same drug that he'd used on her parents.

She felt cold as her muscles numbed further, but there was no pain. That thought comforted Dana as her mind dragged her toward the darkness. If this was how her parents had gone, at least they hadn't suffered. At least she wouldn't suffer.

Just as the last pinprick of light faded, Jake popped into her thoughts. His pained blue eyes haunted her as she wondered how much he would suffer if he survived this mess she'd dragged him into.

46

Watery light filtered through closed curtains, but even that was enough to sting Jake's eyes. He blinked trying to clear the fogginess from his mind. When the unfamiliar room finally came into focus, he realized where he was with a sudden start. Twin beds, nightstand, lamp, dresser, TV ... he'd woken in a murder scene. Or what was about to be one.

"Over my dead body," Jake muttered.

He tried to wake his sluggish limbs, but they were still unresponsive. Even if they weren't, the restraints strapping him to the bed made sure he wasn't going anywhere. As he shook off the cobwebs in his mind, any hope that this was just a bad dream vanished. Jake could feel the tight straps biting into his skin. Instinct made his heartbeat race in his temples, but he fought against his panic. He'd been trained for this, and in a matter of moments his military conditioning kicked in.

Deep breathing slowed his pulse, allowing him the space he needed to think this situation through. Desperation wouldn't free him any faster. He needed logic and strategic measures if he was going to save himself and Dana from the madman who had them in his sights.

Regret stretched across his chest tighter than his restraints as his mind flashed back to his mistake at the airport. He'd never forgive himself if Dana suffered because of his carelessness. But he'd been in such a rush to get back to her that he hadn't been as vigilant as he should. That had allowed someone to get the drop on him in the parking lot.

The guy was on Jake before he had a moment to react. He assumed his hooded attacker was Cramer. He was the right build, but he couldn't be sure. He hadn't seen much thanks to the harsh glare of the sun. The last thing Jake remembered was the sting of the needle the hooded man plunged into his neck.

Then . . . this.

Jake woke up here, as one half of the final crime scene on Cramer's killing spree.

His eyes traveled to the empty bed next to him. A bed that waited for Dana.

Where the hell was she?

A searing ache built inside of Jake when he imagined what she was going through right now at Cramer's hands. This was all his fault. He should've listened to her and called in backup despite the risks. It might have sent Cramer into the wind, but at least Dana would've been safe.

Why the hell did Jake have to make everything personal?

Even after all these years, he'd learned nothing. If he hadn't been adamant about being the one to take down his mentor, Jake wouldn't be strapped to a bed right now, going out of his mind with worry for his partner.

Dana could hold her own; she'd proven that. But Cramer wasn't an ordinary adversary. He had military training and government clearance. That made him nearly unstoppable. Whatever happened now was on Jake. This was why he worked alone. He didn't want to be responsible for someone else's life. Not when he'd proved he couldn't come through when it mattered.

First Ramirez and now Dana ...

Jake struggled against the harsh reality that no matter what he did, he'd never clear his conscience. If Cramer got to Dana, there would be no redemption for him. He'd finally have to admit it; he wasn't worthy of all the things he wanted. Redemption. Forgiveness. Love.

Love ... The idea made Jake want to laugh.

Who would ever be so foolish to crave something so fragile in a world as sinister as this one? Especially at a time like this?

Jake was strapped to a mattress, counting down the minutes he had left before his homicidal boss showed up to end his joke of a life. It didn't get much darker than that. And Jake knew darkness. Hell, he'd played a part in adding more of it to the world. He knew better than to ever hope he could deserve the things he craved.

Maybe his CO had been right in Ghazni. Jake should've saved everyone the trouble and just ate his gun after tanking their mission.

Jake's adrenaline surged, his ego fighting back against his depressing thoughts. He was no coward. And he wasn't throwing in the towel until there was nothing left to fight for. And for Dana, he would fight until his last breath. Someone should.

Cramer had taken away her family. He'd stolen years of unconditional love only parents could give. No matter what happened here, Jake couldn't give her that back. But he could at least fight hard enough to show her she wasn't alone in their final hours.

Slowing his inhale, Jake concentrated on deep breathing, forcing oxygen into his bloodstream to overcome the poison's grip. He didn't know what he'd been drugged with or how long it would last, but he could already feel his outer extremities beginning to tingle back to life. With any luck, it was nightshade and Jake could beat the half-life of the sedative so he'd be ready to strike when Cramer arrived. It was a long shot, but Jake was out of options.

47

Fighting the dark places in his mind was almost as difficult for Jake as fighting the poison pulsing through his veins. He'd been in and out of consciousness. There was no clock in the room, and his watch had been removed, but he marked the passage of time by the sunlight filtering in through the drawn curtains. The fact that there was none now told Jake that he'd been out for a while.

Wondering what had woken him, he tested his restraints again. They still held strong, but he could feel his muscles tingling back to life.

Hope surged through him, taking solid shape as the door to his room creaked open. Cramer slipped inside, carrying a lifeless looking woman in his arms. *Dana!* Jake held his breath as he watched Cramer gently place her on the empty twin bed. Her motionless form didn't require restraints, but Jake was reassured by the steady rise and fall of her chest. His relief was short-lived. Cramer turned on the lamp and pulled a vial and syringe from his pocket. He placed both on the night-stand between the beds before sitting down next to Dana.

The springs on the bed groaned in protest under the big man's weight, but there was no other noise in the room. Dana didn't recoil or moan as Cramer brushed a gloved hand over her forehead. The gesture was intimate, almost loving. It made Jake's stomach knot. He wanted to slug the guy for putting Dana through even one more moment of torment. The woman's entire life had been dedicated to studying nightmares thanks to him. She didn't need more.

As much as Jake's lungs ached to scream, *keep your hands off her*, he kept his mouth shut, not wanting to blow his cover. If he was going to have any chance of playing the hero today, he was going to have to wait until the last possible moment, giving his muscles as much time as possible to recover before he made his move.

"There, there," Cramer crooned as he arranged Dana neatly on the bed, folding her hands over her chest. "You rest now. It's almost time."

Jake willed himself to remain still while Cramer reached for the syringe, filling it from the vial. He held it up to the yellow lamp light and flicked the air bubbles to the top before expertly increasing the pressure on the plunger just enough to push out the air and not any of the precious drug. Cramer grabbed Dana's slender arm, pushing her sleeve up so he could find a vein. He frowned, quickly putting the needle down on the nightstand next to the vial of poison. Jake's eyes strained to read the label that was now facing him. Ketamine.

Christ! Had Cramer dosed them with Special K?

No wonder Jake felt like a Humvee had run over his mind.

The military had been using ketamine on the front line for ages. Its fast-acting pain killing properties were perfect for battlefield patch jobs. But Jake had seen just what the drug could do in the hands of an expert. His special forces unit used ketamine in interrogations. It was highly effective thanks to its paralytic and hallucinogenic side effects. With the right amount of sleep deprivation and hypnotic suggestions, the drug became a truth serum, making the target putty in an interrogator's hands.

But ketamine was a class three controlled substance. It would definitely show up on a tox screen. This wasn't the drug used on the other victims. If Cramer had switched from nightshade to Special K, it meant he was straying from his normal MO. And that was never a good thing.

Serial Killers were creatures of habit. They only departed from their usual patterns under the most extreme of circumstances, which made them unpredictable, and even more dangerous.

Cramer using ketamine was a bad sign. So was the fact that he'd just removed his gloves. It meant he was no longer afraid of getting caught. An FBI agent with nothing to lose? Jake didn't like his odds, but he reminded himself to hold fast. He'd beat worse foes before, maybe he could do it again.

Jake fixed his eyes on Cramer, not at all liking the worry on the seasoned agent's face. He took off his jacket, removing his weapon and placing it on the nightstand next to the drugs. He climbed back on the bed, this time straddling Dana.

Jake's mind snapped to the worst-case scenario. There was no way he was going to lie there and watch his partner get treated like a date rape victim. Tensing his muscles, Jake balled his hands into fists. He was about to make his move and blow his cover when he realized he'd been wrong about Cramer's motives.

The man wasn't about to assault her, he was trying to save her.

Cramer's ruddy complexion reddened as he applied chest compressions. Winded from the exertion, he paused just long enough to tilt Dana's head back and press his lips to hers, breathing for her, before going back to chest compressions. Jake's own chest felt like it was caving in as he helplessly watched. *Had the dumb bastard overdosed her?*

Jake could no longer remain idle. If Cramer was carrying around a drug as volatile as ketamine, there was also a chance he was carrying the antidote. "Cramer!"

The agent's face whirled in Jake's direction, his gaze wide, almost like he'd forgotten Jake was still in the room. "What did you give her?"

He ignored Jake and went back to CPR. After two more rounds of compressions, he sat back on his heels, winded, but satisfied. Dana's chest rose and fell on its own again. Climbing off her, Cramer went for the syringe again.

"Are you crazy?" Jake snapped. "You'll kill her."

Cramer's dull eyes met Jake's. "That's the plan."

"Why? What the hell did she do to you? Hasn't she already been through enough?"

C.J. CROSS

Cramer's face fell. "Shepard, this isn't a punishment. It's an honor, a privilege, a reprieve."

"It's not one she would choose."

"You know her that well?"

"I know if she wanted to die, she would've made that choice a long time ago, thanks to you."

"You think you figured it out, but you have no idea."

"Then why don't you fill me in?"

"It's too late." Cramer gripped the syringe and turned back to face the bed.

"No! Take me. If you need to take a life, take mine."

Cramer grinned. "I knew I'd made the right choice pairing you with her. I knew you wouldn't be able to resist falling for her. You're so much alike. Two wounded souls convinced you're better off on your own. The perfect pair of star-crossed lovers."

"You don't know what you're talking about."

Cramer tsked. "Always the hero. 'Spare her, take me.' Too bad you didn't make the sacrifice in Ghazni. Then maybe Ramirez would still be here, and you never would've had your little fall from grace that landed you in my lap."

"Just tell me what you want, Cramer. We can work together to make this go away."

"There's no way out now."

"Yes there is. That's the job. Investigate every possible option. You taught me that. You still have options. Just leave her out of this, and I'll do whatever you need me to do."

"Well I'm glad you feel that way." He turned back toward Dana.

"Cramer! Don't do this!"

Throwing Jake one last look, Cramer grinned. "Don't worry. You'll both be together in the end."

This was the moment. Jake had drawn out the sands in the hourglass to the very last grain. He had to act now, or it would be too late. Unleashing his anger, his muscles coiled, responding at last. His hands curled around his restraints and heaved.

214

48

Dana's eyes slit open, her vision dancing with a nightmare as Cramer leaned over her, syringe in hand. She tried to scream, but the sound lodged inside her dry throat, strangled by fear. He smiled at her as he leaned closer, whispering words her mind was too sluggish to understand.

Her head throbbed as her vision toggled between the needle and Cramer's kind expression. The juxtaposition was too much for her drugged state of mind. She blinked fast and hard, trying to make sense of her surroundings, but the next thing that came into view only made her eyes widen further.

A shadow moved behind Cramer.

She realized it was Jake a moment too late, her shocked expression alerting Cramer to the attack. Cramer turned, slamming into Jake with surprising force. Jake staggered back, and that's when Dana saw the syringe. The one that had been meant for her was now sunk deep into Jake's abdomen, the fight slowly draining out of his bright blue eyes, taking Dana's hope with it.

Tears blurred Dana's view of the final killing floor. She'd made herself turn away when Cramer roughly strapped Jake back to the bed.

She didn't want that to be her last memory of him. But she couldn't turn away from the current horror Cramer was searing into her mind.

He stooped low between the beds, painting the floor with painstaking care. The blood he used came from a donor bag, which explained how he'd kept the crime scenes so clean, and why she and Jake had never been able to ID the blood used to make the pentagrams. The one Cramer currently worked on was nearly complete. He worked clockwise starting with the left point and working his way to filling in the bottom point last. "Point thee toward hell and He will justify the unjustifiable."

The lump in Dana's throat grew tighter. Cramer was quoting the *Pentanic Verses*. It was surely a sign of madness if he believed what he'd been doing—what he was about to do—was justifiable. The last shred of hope she'd been clinging to unraveled like a thread being yanked free.

Thanks to whatever Cramer had in the syringe, Jake remained incapacitated. Dana glanced over at him repeatedly to make sure he was still breathing; a ridiculous worry under the circumstances.

Barring a miracle, they'd both be beyond breathing soon enough. But that didn't mean Dana was giving up. It just wasn't in her nature. She'd learned that when she faced Cramer at the café.

She'd always thought solving her parents' murder would give her closure and bring an end to her tireless quest for justice. Sitting across from her parents' killer, Dana had expected to feel peace and exhaustion. Instead, staring into the crazed mind of Thomas Cramer had somehow renewed her will to live.

She refused to give in and let him win. Her love for her parents was stronger than his hate and delusion, and she planned to prove it. If she could stall him long enough to free herself from her restraints, she'd do whatever it took to make sure Cramer was the only one who didn't walk out of this hotel of horrors alive.

Dana wet her lips and began her work. "If I'm going to die, I need to know the truth."

Cramer looked up at her, his gaze curious.

"Why did you pick my parents?"

"They were blessed."

"I don't understand."

"Because you are but a ghost in this realm. But I can fix that." He murmured, going back to painting his masterpiece on the floor while he quietly spoke to himself. "Be still, ghost. Table thy unfinished business, for I am in the business of ushering all things to an end."

He was quoting scripture again. At least it was scripture to him. Cramer had somehow gotten dragged under by the current of the Pentacle Church and unless Dana could find a way to pull him out, she'd never get the truth about her parents.

It was getting late. She didn't have any idea of the time, but she knew hours had passed since she'd been with Cramer in the café. If she could keep him talking a little longer, she was sure the drugs would wear off enough for her to work her hands free. Thinking she wasn't a threat, Cramer only tied her wrists. While she'd been talking, and he'd been busy perfecting his bloody pentagram, she'd been working the knot. They were almost loose enough to slip. She just needed a little longer.

"How long have you been with them?" she asked. "The Pentacle Church."

Cramer nodded while he worked. "A long time."

"Is your brother with the church, too?"

Cramer's gaze flicked up to meet hers, his lips twitching into a frown. "He was."

"Was?"

"The world is a place proven real by dying in it."

Dana's heart thundered in her eardrums. Was Cramer's brother dead? Is that what Jake had found out on his trip? If so, it was the exact type of trigger he'd warned her could cause a psychotic break like this. Dana racked her brain for his name. Finding it, she clutched it like a life raft. "Rycroft wouldn't want you to do this."

Cramer shook his head, his dry lips stretching into a grin so wide Dana feared they'd crack. "Rycroft taught me how to free the demons inside us. He taught me how to be reborn."

Tears filled Dana's eyes. "Did he teach my parents that too?"

Cramer's grin spread wider as he nodded. "He chose to help them, to free their madness. Theirs were the first souls I freed. And now I will free you."

Dana's tears flowed freely now. This man was insane. There was no reasoning with him and no way to decipher the truth from his rantings. She would never know if her parents' death had been random or if they too had been somehow tied up in this cult. Her heart wouldn't let her believe the latter. That would destroy her life's purpose.

She'd spent her life studying the occult, thinking it would give her answers, but what if all it did was lead her down the same path her parents had taken? A path with no answers. A path of death that only led to more death.

As Dana lay there, struggling to free herself, she sank into the dark corners of her mind, finally asking the questions she normally kept at bay. If this was how it ended, had her life been wasted? Would her parents be disappointed in her? Did her obsession with finding the truth lead her to the same demise? And did that make it all for nothing?

All at once, Dana felt the effects of the drugs subsiding. Her gaze darted from Cramer to the nightstand. The drugs, syringe and his handgun were still there. Glancing back at Cramer, she contemplated her half-baked plan. It was risky considering her track record with firearms, but she refused to go down without a fight.

When she glanced back at the gun, a twitch of movement in her peripheral caught her attention. She held her breath as she watched Jake, waiting for another sign of life. This time his twitch was accompanied with a wink.

Dana's heart nearly burst when she saw his stormy blue eyes flash open. He gave a brief nod to the gun on the dresser, but Dana had already made up her mind. They all stood a better chance if she went for the poison. Knowing Jake was at least coherent enough to get the hell out of there if her plan worked gave Dana all the courage she needed to make her move.

With one massive surge of adrenaline, she slipped her wrists free and lunged for the nightstand. The syringe was already in her hand by the time Cramer realized what was happening, but he moved with the speed of a man possessed.

Dana didn't let him intimidate her.

She stood her ground, ready to jam the drug into his neck. She knew she'd only get one shot at this. But Cramer came at her too fast.

When he was close enough for her to strike, he struck first. His fist connected with her jaw so hard she saw stars. To her credit, she never let go of the needle. She swung it wildly, trying to get it into his system anyway possible as his arms tried to restrain her.

In the struggle, she caught Jake out of the corner of her eye, trying to break free of his restraints, but his straps held fast. Dana's brief distraction proved dire. Her momentary glance at Jake had given Cramer the time he needed to intercept her move. His hand shot out, blocking the arc of her arm as she aimed the syringe at the powerful meat of his thigh. She'd probably telegraphed her path, but either way, Cramer was ready for her. His fist blocked the blow, the tip of the needle bending against his knuckle before breaking and dropping uselessly to the floor.

Cramer's arms came around her. One coiling around her neck, restricting her air supply, the other around her torso. Dana pivoted in his arms until their eyes met, deadlocked in a silent standoff before she made her final move. It was the only one she had left.

Going limp, she used her full body weight to throw him off balance before stepping as hard as she could on his tender instep. Then she twisted, tucked her knees, and lifted both feet so she could kick off the nightstand.

Everything went flying. Cramer. Dana. The gun. The drugs. Jake's shouts were the only thing that kept Dana moving. She climbed to her feet moments before Cramer and raced toward the nightstand, but the gun was gone. Tossed somewhere in her frantic attempt to take the big man down.

"Dana!" Jake shouted. "Forget the gun. My straps."

She reached his side, grabbing hold of the strap at the same time Cramer grabbed her ankle. Both yanked. Only time would tell which side fate favored.

Dana's eyes met Jake's for a moment before she was ripped away, her fingernails dragging across the carpet until they tore away from her nail beds. She screamed and thrashed, making as much noise as she could. If there was anyone else in the hotel, she was making damn sure they were going to hear her. This fight was no longer just Dana's. Cramer had brought an entire satanic cult with him. It was about time she made this a fair fight.

Rolling on top of him, she kneed him in the crotch. It gave her time to get up, but Cramer was unstoppable. He kicked out and swept her legs. Dana went down hard, the wind rushing out of her lungs. She gasped for air, giving Cramer time to get to his feet. She scuttled backwards like a crab, but it was no use. Cramer reached down and hauled her up by her hair. Her scream was silenced as Cramer's arms encircled her again, his forearm crushing her windpipe once more.

Suddenly the room fell silent, except for the unmistakable click of a bullet sliding into the chamber.

Cramer whirled toward the sound, putting Dana squarely between him and the barrel of the gun Jake now held. Dana's eyes watered as she met Jake's furious gaze. "Let her go," Jake commanded.

But Cramer had other plans. He pulled a knife from his belt and raised it to Dana's face, pressing the cold steel just below her jaw. Her pulse rebelled against the pressure of the blade, throbbing furiously as if to say, *go ahead, you can kill me, but you can't kill what I stand for.*

Dana wished she was as brave as her defiant heartbeat, but this was not the end she'd envisioned. Even so, it was here, and she had to face it. At least this way, one of them would leave the hotel room alive.

Dana's eyes met Jake's one last time. She knew she wasn't going to survive this, but Jake still could. She took a deep breath, memorizing his face before she whispered the only thing left to do. "Take the shot."

49

Jake's voice was as rough as gravel as he growled at his former boss. "Let her go, Cramer."

"I am but a tool waking the world from its slumber."

Jake had been waiting, praying for the crazy to drain out of Cramer's expression so he'd know his friend was still in there, but there were no traces left of the man Jake thought he knew. Cramer had dissolved into pure lunacy, ranting his satanic babble. But Jake refused to believe all was lost.

How many times had he and Ramirez been in situations that seemed hopeless? How many times had they walked away?

Jake's mind jumped to that last dark moment, the one where his best friend had not walked away. With a steady breath, Jake pushed the memory away, focusing on the situation in front of him. He willed this outcome to be positive. The same way he willed away Dana's suicidal tendencies.

There was no way he was taking the shot. Not when Cramer was using her as a human shield. He just needed a moment to think without watching the glint of the knife pressed against Dana's delicate flesh or listening to her silently begging him to end this as Cramer inched closer and closer toward the door.

Even if he had a clean shot to take, death was too swift a mercy for Cramer. Despite all the evil he'd witnessed, Jake still believed in the justice system. He wanted to let the good men and women he worked with have a chance to unravel this monster for no other reason than to find out how many other victims there were. Their families deserved justice. The same justice Dana was trying to exact with her own self-sacrifice.

Jake shut everything out, everything but Dana's voice. Something she'd said about Ramirez drifted back to him. *Maybe he's looking down on you now, a guardian angel guiding you.*

Jake wanted so badly for that to be true. Ramirez had been his ride or die. Together, they'd faced situations much worse and always found a way to come out on the other side. *Not always,* his guilty conscience reminded him.

Jake pushed away the thought, letting himself imagine for a moment that Dana was right. That Ramirez was just out of sight, waiting in the wings like always to guide Jake safely home, should he need it. If Ramirez was here, he'd help Jake come up with a plan to take down Cramer. He'd give a wink or a nod, tell some inside joke that would remind Jake of a play they'd run in Kabul or some other far corner of the world.

That's when it came to him. Kabul. The first time Jake had taken a bullet, courtesy of his best friend.

He heard Ramirez's voice as clear as day. *If you can't go around, go through.*

Without warning, Jake moved his finger from the guard to the trigger and squeezed on his exhale. Gunfire burst through the room, but Jake was unfazed by the deafening sound. He was moving as the bodies fell, but not fast enough.

Dana hit the floor, but Cramer managed to stay on his feet. He'd been thrown into the door and from the smear of blood on it, he'd been hit, just as Jake planned. But so had Dana. That had also been an unavoidable part of his plan, but he hesitated chasing Cramer to make sure his aim was true.

"Breathe," he ordered, as he knelt next to her.

She hissed when his hands reached the wound in her shoulder. It was clean. A through and through, just as he planned. Jake's finger traced her cheek before checking her pulse at her carotid. He gazed into her wide pupils, making sure she wasn't in shock. Surprisingly, she was holding her own.

"You good?" he asked, gently.

Dana nodded. "I'm fine. Don't lose him!" she ordered once she regained her breath.

Jake pulled her to her feet. "Stay here."

"Not a chance!"

Dana probably still had enough ketamine in her system to dull the full effects of her injury. She'd feel it soon enough, but until then, the only place Jake wanted her was by his side. Grabbing a clean towel for her wound, he met her fierce gaze. "We do this together."

Dana nodded. "Together."

"Stick by my side."

50

"I HIT HIM," JAKE YELLED AS THEY RAN FROM THE HOTEL ROOM FOLLOWING Cramer's trail of blood.

"Not mortally I hope," Dana snapped.

Jake cut his eyes at her. "You're the one who told me to take the shot."

"And I'm glad you did, but if he dies, the truth about my parents dies with him."

Jake picked up his pace, each footstep slapping the pavement, a vow to get her answers. She was grateful and did her best to keep up with him, but her shoulder burned.

The events of the past few hours were taking their toll. Dana cashed in her fading reserves of adrenaline as she followed Jake out of the hotel, through the parking lot and into the alley. There was nowhere to run down here. But if Dana knew that, so did Cramer. Like a rat returning to the sewer, he was coming home to die.

The hotel Cramer had chosen for his final sacrifice was in a seedy part of the city. The urban landscape worked against him. His bloody footprints were easy to track on the concrete.

Jake shouted codes into his phone as he called in the shooting while they raced after Cramer. She heard him request an ambulance, but she wondered who it was for. By the amount of blood on the ground, she worried Cramer would bleed out before they could get to him. That's when Dana saw him. A dark shadow slumped against the damp brick wall. She sped up, but Jake reached a hand out, stopping her. He drew his weapon and pulled Dana behind him.

"Thomas Cramer, you're under arrest for the murders of James and Renee Gray ..."

Dana didn't hear the rest of the names that followed her parents' as Jake rattled off the list of victims this man and his brother had senselessly snuffed out in the name of some misguided religion. She was no longer hearing or seeing. Her heart was too consumed with pain as she stepped around Jake.

Cramer was helpless now. There was nothing he could do to hurt her that he hadn't already done. He slouched against the decrepit building in a crumpled heap, his legs sprawled out in front of him like a marionette without strings. Cramer wheezed as Dana knelt next to him to watch the life slowly drain out of his hateful eyes. With each futile pump of his heart, blood oozed from the bullet wound in his chest. "I hope it hurts like hell," she whispered.

"Death is but a fall into the next life."

"There is no life where you're going," she hissed, holding back the sting of tears. "You killed my parents and God knows how many innocent people."

"God has nothing to do with it," he interrupted.

"You're right. Some evil is too much for any god to overcome. The only comfort I have is knowing that when you take your last breath, this evil you spread dies with you."

Cramer gave a gurgling laugh. "Do you really think I acted alone? This isn't over. Death is just the beginning."

Cramer's eyes closed and Dana fought the chill that settled deep in her bones. A hand brushed her shoulder, and she turned to meet Jake's sympathetic gaze. Embarrassed by her brief and uncontrolled wrath, she wondered how much of her final conversation with Cramer he'd overheard.

When Jake reached his hand out to her, there was no judgement in his eyes. She realized whatever he'd heard didn't matter to him. That level of acceptance made her chest feel tight. She took his hand, letting his warmth wrap around her as he pulled her to her feet and into his embrace.

"This isn't over, is it?" she whispered into his shoulder.

"It is for now."

Dana buried her face into Jake's chest, trying to hide the angry tears burning her eyes. "But we didn't get any answers."

Jake gently gripped her good shoulder, guiding her back so he could look into her eyes. The intensity she found in his gaze made her ache for all the wrong reasons. "We know more than we did yesterday. Sometimes, that's all we get." His fingertips softly brushed back the hair matted to her cheeks by tears and sweat. "Sometimes, that has to be enough."

"But it's not. It's not even close to enough."

"I know."

"So what do you do then?"

Dark emotions swirled behind his turbulent blue gaze for a moment before he offered her a faint smile. "You wake up tomorrow and try again." Jake squeezed the tension in her good shoulder. "Come on, let's go get you patched up, partner."

Dana nodded, giving one last look over her shoulder at the lifeless man who'd taken so much from her. As she turned away, walking toward the flashing blue and red lights, she decided Jake was right. What they'd accomplished today would have to be enough—for now.

She lifted her chin a little higher, knowing she'd not only rid the world of a tiny drop of evil, but she'd faced her biggest fear, and most importantly, lived to fight another day.

51

Dana winced as she adjusted her sling.

The doctor told her she'd make a full recovery, but the gunshot wound still ached. Though not nearly as bad as her heart.

Her bruises had healed, but there was a part of her that would never recover from the events of the past few weeks. The only way she'd made it this far was thanks to Jake and Claire.

They'd both doted on her after her injury. *Ghostbuster* movie marathons, endless Thai takeout, and their constant hovering had nearly smothered her. And though she'd fought them every step of the way, knowing she had people in her life who she could count on meant more than she could ever say.

Dana's chest tightened as she watched the scene unfolding over the cartons of takeout boxes. She'd gotten used to having Jake around like this, for meals and conversation. She even enjoyed it. And it was clear Claire did too as she squealed with delight, watching Jake pucker his lips in disgust when she told him exactly what was in his dumpling.

"Brains! You made me eat brains!"

"Who knows, it might make you smart enough to work here one day," Claire teased.

Jake used his chopsticks to make an obscene gesture that made Claire laugh even harder. It was a sound Dana could get used to.

She would miss this; the cheery way Jake filled her office. But at the same time, she was ready for her life to return to normal.

It'd been more than two weeks since they'd taken Cramer down and solved the Romeo and Juliet murders. Endless days of meetings, depositions and statements bled together until finally the FBI was satisfied and the case was officially closed. That's what today's celebration dinner was about. One more meal in what had become "their place."

Dana looked around the lab, wondering if her library would feel different once Jake left for good. She reminded herself that's what she wanted. Her life back. Her quiet, ordinary life. One where FBI agents didn't pop in and drape badges and gun belts over her precious books and disrupt the natural order of things. Jake belonged in the J. Edgar Hoover Building. Dana belonged in her library.

Even though she was eager to return to the safety of her routine, she could admit saying goodbye was harder than she'd expected. Jake Shepard had grown on her. She told herself it was just the intensity of what they'd endured working the case together that bonded them, but if she were being honest, it was more than that. At least it could be if she'd let it.

The gruff FBI agent had somehow gotten past her defenses. And she felt like, just maybe, she'd done the same to him.

Jake's gaze flashed to hers, his expression a mirror of her own. Was he reluctant to see this end too? She saw a lot of herself in him. They were both flawed, but resilient, and that made her realize she was less alone in the world than she thought. Dana would always be grateful to Jake for showing her that. But the case was over. It was time to move on.

They'd both done their jobs and defeated the enemy. There was no reason for their paths to continue to align. Again, she reminded herself, that was a good thing. What happened with Cramer was all the proof she needed. Dana didn't belong in Jake's world. She'd almost gotten them both killed trying to take justice into her own hands.

Everything she'd been through on this case reaffirmed her beliefs.

Dana's place was here, at the Smithsonian. It was where she could make a difference.

Another thing working with Jake had taught her was that her work was important. Even though she'd gotten as close as she ever would to finding out what happened to her parents, her work wasn't finished. There was still so much in the occult world left to uncover. And Dana wasn't the only survivor left behind with questions. She had to continue her work to get a better understanding of the occult world, to find answers to all the unexplainable phenomenon and misunderstood rituals. If she could explain them in black and white, maybe there would be less dark misinterpretation, less death and destruction.

It was a worthy calling to dedicate her life to, and one best tackled on her own.

Not one to prolong the inevitable, Dana cleaned up her takeout box and stood. Jake caught her movement and paused his conversation with Claire. Their eyes met, and he gave Dana a nod of understanding. Rising, he walked over to Claire and gave her shoulder a squeeze. "Take care, kid. And make sure you leave some dumplings at Thaiphoon for me."

Claire surprised Dana by jumping to her feet and wrapping her arms around Jake. He seemed as shocked as Dana, but he recovered quickly, wrapping Claire in a tight but brief hug. Clearing his throat, he stepped back. "I'll see ya around, Elvira."

Dana's misty-eyed intern sniffled. "Stay safe, Secret Agent Man."

Jake winked and turned to face Dana as he grabbed his things. "Walk me out?"

She nodded, giving one last look around her crowded office before their misfit family would disband for good.

52

THE DC WEATHER MATCHED JAKE'S MOOD—ICY AND BLEAK. IT FELT wrong to be walking away from this woman. But their case was over. He had no reason to stay. Well, no reasons he was willing to admit. What would be the point of telling Dana he didn't want this to end? What would he even say? *This has been fun, let's do it again sometime? Hardly.*

But still, the idea of Dana not being in his future made it feel so pointless. Dana had been a bright spot in Jake's otherwise murky existence. She'd burst into his life like a wrecking ball, breaking down his walls until she was under his skin. He'd hated it at first, but now ... now he didn't know how to let her go. But he had to. For both their sakes. He'd hurt or disappointed everyone he'd ever gotten close to. Dana would be no different. It was better to cut ties now before he got in too deep.

"I have something for you." Jake pulled a jump drive from his pocket and handed it to Dana.

"What is it?"

"It's your parents' case file." It was actually more than that. The jump drive also contained the recent evidence the FBI had collected from Rycroft Cramer's property, including the developed film pertaining to her parents.

It didn't make up for all that had been taken from Dana, but it was a small act and one she deserved.

Her brown eyes filled with emotion. "I thought this was government property?"

"I pulled some strings." He shrugged. "It was the least I could do."

"Jake ... I don't know what to say."

"You don't have to say anything. Just promise me you won't let what happened to them define you."

Dana's eyes watered with unshed tears. Jake had to look away. If she cried, he'd cave and pull her into his arms, saying all the things he'd promised himself he wouldn't. He kicked the cold concrete sidewalk like a damn teenager as he reeled in his emotions.

"Dana, I hope you know we never would've gotten Cramer without you. And it's because of you that his victims' families have closure." His gaze met hers again. "The work you do is important. I'm sorry I didn't see that at first. I hope you stick with it."

"I plan to."

"Good." He nodded, exhaling deeply.

"What about you?"

"What about me?"

"You're staying with the FBI?"

He nodded. It hadn't been an easy decision, but in the end, he still believed he was doing good. "They're not all like Cramer."

"I know."

"Plus, they gave me a few extra weeks paid vacation. I think I'm gonna head down to the Keys. Might even try to convince my uncle to join me."

"That sounds nice."

An awkward silence stretched out between them. If Jake didn't say goodbye now, he'd end up asking her to come to Florida with him. "Well, I guess this is goodbye."

Dana stuck her hand out, all business as usual. "It's been a pleasure."

"The pleasure was all mine." He savored the feel of her hand in his for a moment longer than necessary before letting go. "Goodbye, Dana. Take care of yourself."

"You too, Agent Shepard."

Hearing his formal name was a tiny dagger to Jake's heart, but he supposed he should get used to it.

This is for the best, he reminded himself as he walked toward the parking lot.

He had no business getting involved with anyone. Not when his job required him to balance on the knife's edge of justice. Jake couldn't afford to be distracted. And he was already distracted enough by all the past wrongs he had to right.

Even knowing all of this, it didn't make walking away from Dana any easier.

Jake knew she was still standing there, staring after him. He could feel the pull of her under his skin.

Impulsively, he turned around, cursing himself before the words were even out of his mouth. If she turned him down, his already bruised ego would shatter. But he asked anyway. "I'm not saying I'm asking, but if the situation ever arose, could I call on you to help me with a case again?"

Dana crossed her arms tightly over her chest. "Since you're not asking, I'm not answering."

"Fair enough." Jake's confidence deflated. What had he expected with that half-assed proposal? He should've left well enough alone. Jake forced a grin that felt more like a grimace, ready to leave for good this time.

Then Dana smiled. "That wasn't a no."

"Roger that." Jake gave a quick salute, then turned to walk away before Dana got a glimpse of the smile he couldn't scrub off his face if he tried.

He didn't know when their paths would cross again, but for now, the door was open, and that was enough.

53

Dana stood outside until Jake got into his SUV and drove off.

She wrapped her arms around herself to stave off the cold, watching him vanish in the distance. When his taillights disappeared into the busy DC traffic, she turned to head back inside, rubbing warmth back into her limbs as she climbed into the tomb-like elevator that carried her below ground where her work waited.

During her slow descent, she thought of the man she'd just watched walk away from her.

Strangely, a smile tugged at her lips, because this time, being left behind didn't feel like an ending, but rather the beginning of something bigger than she'd ever imagined.

Did you enjoy reading **Girl Left Behind**? We would love to hear about it! Please consider leaving a review here:

https://www.amazon.com/review/B098KGXC2G

The story continues in Girl on the Hill. Read on for an excerpt, or order your copy now:

https://www.amazon.com/gp/product/B098KHCXRT

GIRL ON THE HILL: CHAPTER 1

"Why are you staring at me like I'm one of your crusty old books that you're trying to decode?" Jake asked.

Dana tilted her head. "Because you look different."

Jake couldn't help himself. He'd missed her more than he should and now that they were finally back together, he couldn't seem to rein in his flirtation. "Good, different?"

"Tan, different."

He laughed. "Well, Florida does that to a person."

"So you enjoyed Key West?"

"Everyone enjoys Key West. Palm trees, sunshine, piña coladas. It's paradise. I'd move there in a heartbeat."

"Why don't you?"

"'Cause I still have work to do here. Like teaching you how to shoot. Come on, you have to hit the target at least once before we call it a day."

Jake sent the untouched paper target back down the lane and reloaded his Sig Sauer 9mm. "Square up."

Dana pulled her ear protection back in place and did as instructed. Her long brown hair was pulled into a ponytail. It swayed down her back as she moved into her shooting stance. Even with her safety glasses on, she still somehow managed to be the best thing Jake had laid eyes on in months.

A few weeks of vacation had turned into a few months. Key West had no shortage of gorgeous women, and Jake had enjoyed himself with a few, but none of them were Dr. Dana Gray.

That was the problem, and partly why Jake had extended his vacation. He'd been trying to get the sexy librarian out of his head. They weren't partners anymore, no matter how much he might want her to be. But he couldn't blame her. Their last case had even made Jake reassess his commitment to the FBI.

Ultimately, he still felt he had unfinished business to atone for. But it was different for Dana. She wasn't an agent. She'd only been consulting on the case, and it had almost gotten her killed. He understood why she wouldn't be eager to go down that road again.

He told himself it was for the best. Dana was a distraction. And distractions in his line of work could be deadly. But here he was, appreciating her ass when he was supposed to be correcting her form.

Jake had only been back in DC for two weeks before he caved and called Dana, using these promised shooting lessons as an excuse to see her. But then again, if her aim hadn't been so bad, she might've ended their last case before things got so out of hand.

Refocusing, Jake nudged Dana's stance wider, tapping his shoe against her boots. He moved his hands to her hips and shifted her balance back into her seat. "Now bend your knees a little. That's it."

Feeling her warm body against his was testing his willpower, but he fought through his desire, determined not to be another person to take advantage of Dana.

She deserved better.

Certainly better than him.

Reminding himself of that, Jake brought his hands up, correcting Dana's grip and lowering her arms a bit more. "Okay. Now pull in a breath and squeeze the trigger on your exhale. Three round bursts in one breath, like I taught you."

Dana gave a slight nod and Jake stepped back, giving her the lane. He watched her shoulders rise on the inhale and relax momentarily before she discharged the weapon. Three shots in succession, just like he'd instructed. And this time, she nicked the target. Dana whirled around with a squeal of delight. "I did it!"

Jake reflexively moved for the gun. Pointing it down-range until the safety was on. He holstered it and grinned. "Nicely done. A few more lessons and you might be able to hit the broad side of a barn."

She cut her eyes at him, before striking out with a playful right hook meant for his shoulder. He dodged it and pulled her into his arms instead. For a moment, they were both caught by surprise. Dana gazed up at him, her brown eyes full of questions. He could feel her heart beating against his chest.

How many nights had he'd ached to have her in his arms like this? Had she thought about him, too? He had to know. His whole body was vibrating with anticipation as he gathered his nerves to just man up and ask her already.

"Jake?"

Dana's voice brought him back to reality. "Yeah?"

"Your phone's ringing."

"Oh. Right." He cleared his throat and straightened. Backing away until he had enough space to think straight. It had been his phone buzzing. *Moron.* He swallowed his embarrassment and answered the call. "Agent Shepard."

He listened intently as his new supervisor filled him in on a missing person case. "I know you're still settling in, but we could really use your help on this one. It's high profile, and I don't want to see it get out of hand. The more eyes we can get on this, the better. I want to get ahead of the press."

Jake agreed. "Text me the address. I'll head there now."

"Report back to me ASAP."

"Roger that."

Jake hung up and turned to face Dana. She was already putting her jacket on. "Sounds like shooting lessons are over for today."

"Yeah. Missing person case just came in."

"I'm sorry."

"Yeah, these are never easy."

"I know."

Their eyes met. Of course, she did. Dana had been through more than her fair share of heartache. "It'll be strange not having you in the field with me. You're good at it. Ever think about a career change?"

She shook her head. "I'm done with that, Jake."

"You sure? We've proved we work well together."

"I'm sure. I'll stick to my area of expertise."

Jake nodded, but he couldn't fight his disappointment. He knew it was for the best that Dana wouldn't be involved in another high stakes FBI case. He cared about her too much as it was. A little distance would be safer for both of them. "Need a lift back to the Smithsonian?"

"No, the weather's nice for a change. I'd rather walk."

"All right." They walked the short way to the exit together. "This case is probably going to keep me wrapped up for a while. But I'll touch base when I resurface."

Dana's hand caught his as he turned away. "Jake ..."

"Yeah?"

She gave his hand a squeeze. "Take care of yourself."

He grinned faintly. "Always do."

GIRL ON THE HILL: CHAPTER 2

"Dr. Fredrick?" Dana couldn't hide the shock in her voice at seeing her boss in her office when she returned to the Smithsonian. She didn't get many visitors on her library level of occult studies. "Is there something I can do for you?"

"I'm not sure there's anything anyone can do."

Dana shrugged off her coat and hung it on the antique Alcott in her office, gesturing for her boss to have a seat, while she took up the worn leather one behind her ornate fourth century desk. "What's this about?"

"The Kincaids."

The name needed no other explanation. Everyone in DC knew the Kincaids and their wealth. Archer and Elizabeth Kincaid were the Smithsonian's largest donors. It was no wonder Dana's boss looked so distraught. He was probably preparing for a visit, or maybe the Kincaids wanted to host another gala at the museum. Dana knew how stressful it could be trying to impress such a prestigious family. They may be intimidating, but to Dana they didn't seem so bad. Mostly because she'd befriended their eldest daughter, Meredith, during her summer internship at the Smithsonian a few years back.

"Do you need help preparing something for the Kincaids?"

"No, the opposite, actually. I'm afraid I have some bad news."

Dana frowned. "I don't understand."

Dr. Fredrick sighed, pinching the bridge of his nose. "I don't know how to tell you this. I know you're close to the family, so I wanted you to hear this from me first. Their daughter's been abducted."

Dana's stomach dropped. "Meredith?"

"Yes."

"When?"

"I don't have all the details. Just that the FBI has officially taken over the case. Are you still in touch with Agent Shepard? He might know more than I do."

Dana nodded. "I'll check with him."

"Please do. And keep me informed." Dr. Fredrick stood. "My heart just breaks for that family. Meredith was such a sweet girl."

"Is," Dana corrected. "Meredith *is* a sweet girl." She reached across the desk and squeezed her boss's hand. "We'll get her back."

Dana would make sure of it.

She wasn't invested because Meredith was some rich donor's daughter, she wanted to find her because they were friends. Or at least the closest Dana had come to having a friend until Shepard walked into her life.

With Dr. Fredrick's footsteps fading further and further away, Dana's mind filled with memories of her missing friend.

Meredith Kincaid had interned at the Smithsonian a few years ago during summer break from college. Dana had gladly taken the bright young girl under her wing. They were only a few years apart and had gotten along fabulously. She remembered late night movies, philosophizing about politics over wine and popcorn and sneaking into the museum after hours to play tourist.

Of course, they hadn't been doing anything illegal.

Dana had a key to the Smithsonian, but it made Meredith so excited to think she was getting away with something. The girl had a rebellious streak. *Had she taken it too far?*

Shepard's offer itched beneath Dana's skin. What was she waiting for? She knew there was no way she could sit this one out. Picking up her phone, she dialed his number from memory.

"Dana? Everything okay?"

"Not really."

"What's wrong?"

"Is your missing person Meredith Kincaid?"

"How did you know that?"

"Does your offer to help with the case still stand?"

"Yes."

"Good. Because I've changed my mind."

"Dana. What aren't you telling me?"

"Pick me up, and I'll tell you everything."

Dana opened the desk drawer. The temporary badge was right where she'd left it. She kept it as a souvenir. But apparently her work with the FBI wasn't over yet.

Enjoying Girl on the Hill? Download your copy today!:
https://www.amazon.com/gp/product/B098KHCXRT

ALSO BY C.J. CROSS

Dana Gray Mysteries

Girl Left Behind

Girl on the Hill

Girl in the Grave

Stay up to date with C.J. Cross's new releases and download her **free** Dana Gray Prequel, *Girl Awakened* by heading to the link:

Find more C.J. Cross books and follow her on Amazon today!

ALSO BY WITHOUT WARRANT

More Thriller Series from Without Warrant Authors

Kenzie Gilmore Thrillers by Biba Pearce

Afterburn

Dead Heat

Heatwave

Burnout

ABOUT THE AUTHOR

CJ Cross grew up in a snowy little Northeast town, cutting her teeth on true crime novels to stave her love of all things mysterious. The writing bug bit her early and she found her way into the publishing world, writing 50+ books under various top secret pen names over the years.

Now relocated to a place where she can safely trade in her snowshoes for flip flops, she's found a reason to dust off her old Criminal Justice degree and she's turned an old passion into a new flame, writing compelling thrillers novels.

When she's not writing you can usually find her drinking bourbon with fellow authors or spoiling her rescue pup.

Sign up for C.J.'s newsletter and download her free **Dana Gray Prequel,** *Girl Awakened*:

https://liquidmind.media/cj-cross-sign-up-1-prequel-download